Breaching the Barriers

A collection of short stories and essays from India

Richard Rose

Cyberwit.net
HIG 45 Kaushambi Kunj, Kalindipuram
Allahabad - 211011 (U.P.) India
http://www.cyberwit.net
Tel: +(91) 9415091004
E-mail: info@cyberwit.net

Printed at Repro India Limited.

Other Books by the Author

Fiction

No Strangers Here. (a collection of short stories)

Poetry

A Sense of Place.

For Performance

Letters to Lucia. (Written with James Vollmar)

On Education and Children's Rights

Establishing Pathways to Inclusion. (with Michael Shevlin)

Assessment for Learning in Inclusive Schools. (with Roar Engh)

Confronting Obstacles to Inclusion.

Count Me In. (with Michael Shevlin)

Encouraging Voices. (with Michael Shevlin)

Strategies to Promote Inclusive Practice. (with Cristina Tilstone)

Promoting Inclusive Practice. (with Cristina Tilstone and Lani Florian) (winner of the NASEN TES Prize)

Introduction

Kicking Against the Barriers

In 2005 my wife Sara and I rode our well-laden bicycles, carrying a tent, cooking equipment and all the paraphernalia necessary for a three week cycle tour around Lake Constance, otherwise known as the Bodensee, Europe's third largest lake. Starting our ride in Friedrichshafen in Germany, we circumnavigated the lake and made occasional detours into the hinterland to explore the magnificent countryside and visit places of historic and artistic interest. This was one of many such excursions that we have made by bicycle to various parts of Europe over the years, and we were well versed in navigating the smallest lanes we could find, travelling at a leisurely pace with regular stops for refreshments, sightseeing and locating quiet campsites. During our many trips by bicycle we have met interesting people, enjoyed local cuisine, and gained a host of memorable experiences. But it was one specific occurrence during this journey through the three countries bordering the Bodensee that prompted me to think about the nature of nationhood and our strange relationship with borders and identity.

The incident occurred well into our journey on a day when we had decided to pedal away from the shoreline of the great lake in search of quiet lanes, and the picturesque villages that typify the region. It was a warm day, and as has often been our habit, late in the morning we looked for a café with outdoor tables where we could enjoy coffee and cakes. These are plentiful across European tourist areas and we had no difficulty on the morning in question in locating an ideal situation where we could sit and look out over the activities of a pleasant village square, whilst enjoying our refreshments. As expected, a friendly waiter arrived at our table and took our order, speaking German, a language in which I can manage the basic necessities for a trip of this nature. An hour later, having enjoyed our break it was time to move on and I called for the bill which was duly delivered to the table. Without much thought about the likely total due, I placed a 20 euro note on the plate, knowing that this would more than cover the costs. I was therefore somewhat surprised when staring at the money offered with obvious distain, the waiter refused to accept payment with an emphatic "nein, wir akzeptieren nicht!" (no, we don't accept). Seeing the look of confusion on my face, and clearly having heard my wife and I conversing in English, he then informed us that "this is Switzerland and here we do not accept the euro."

Sara and I had crossed the border from Austria into Switzerland without any discernible indication that we had changed countries. Indeed, on many occasions when cycling in Europe we have crossed borders without any request for identity or physical notification of entering a new jurisdiction. Recognising our error in assuming that we were still within the eurozone, I apologised profusely and having gained information from the waiter, left Sara seated at our table (as a form of surety) while I cycled a few miles to a local bank with an ATM, in order to obtain some Swiss Francs.

On returning to the café and paying the outstanding bill in local currency (which felt rather like paying a ransom for the release of my wife!), I enquired about the exact whereabouts of the Austrian border. The waiter pointed along the road from which we had arrived and indicated that it was less than a kilometre, but that distance did not matter. This, he informed me, was most certainly Switzerland.

Over the years that have passed since this strange scenario, we have often laughed about this experience and the bizarre nature of the situation in which we had found ourselves. One might have thought that being located less than a kilometre from the border of a country where the euro was the currency of exchange, and furthermore being in the midst of an area frequented by many tourists, that there could have been some flexibility over the use of money. In fact there have been other occasions in the non-euro zones of Europe where I have found a willingness to accept this widely used currency without difficulty. Over the next few days while we were in Switzerland we found that many of the shops were more than pleased to accept this foreign money, though we also noted that change was invariably issued in Swiss francs.

The story recounted thus far is of course, quite trivial. But it does relate to a more serious matter that has been to the forefront of my mind when writing the stories and essays contained within this book. It has been my great privilege over many years to travel, often for work, to many different parts of the world. During these trips I have made good friends, seen numerous wonderful sights, experienced a rich and varied literature, music and art and enjoyed local food and drink. I have marvelled at the diversity of languages, struggled with my own limited linguistic abilities and come to admire the skills, knowledge and understanding of those with whom I have worked or met during the course of my travels.

As travellers our attention is inevitably held by the unusual; that which is different from our everyday experiences. Cows wandering gracefully along a main dual carriageway in Bengaluru, the motorcycle rickshaws of Siem Reap, a dragon dance on the streets of Hong Kong, these are sights rarely if ever seen in the English countryside that is my home. Yet behind each of these phenomena there are people who differ very little in their needs, desires and attitudes from those who I encounter everyday on the streets of England. Somewhere along the line, we have chosen to interpret those situations that differ from our everyday understanding as exotic. We often travel to see the sites that have come to represent an image most closely associated with a country; the Hagia Sophia in Istanbul, the Taj Mahal in Agra, the Pyramids of Egypt or Big Ben and the Houses of Parliament in London. At best, these places provide us with an opportunity to learn and to appreciate the history and cultures that have shaped our world. Unfortunately they too often become little more than a tick on a bucket list of must see icons.

Language and culture have shaped national identities from time immemorial. When crossing the English Channel from England to France, a journey of less than 30 miles, I expect to speak French, to travel on the right-hand side of the road and use the euro as currency. When in India, if working in Bengaluru I expect to hear Kannada spoken, and when in Kerala my ears become attuned to Malayalam and in Telangana to Telugu. Kathakali is a traditional form of dance theatre in Kerala, just as Kabuki is in Japan or Randai in Indonesia. These languages and cultural traditions have developed over centuries and are rightly valued and protected by their advocates. It is often these aspects of a country's heritage that attract us as visitors, interested to learn about those histories and traditions that differ from our own. This is a positive feature of national identity and has been important in enabling individuals to develop pride in their country's achievements and unique features.

There are however, less positive aspects to statements of nationality and identity, though these relate less to long held traditions and more to political and socio-economic structures that have been imposed by governments or through imperial rule. My experience at the Swiss border described above has led me to reflect on some of these more negative factors a great deal and has influenced some of my writing in this book.

Throughout the world, where borders have been moved or reinforced, we have seen the development of conflict and the growth of xenophobia. At the extreme we have seen border disputes deteriorating into violence and the promotion of hatred against entire populations who are identified as different and, in many ways, inferior. Examples of this abound and can be seen for example in the construction of walls between Israel and Palestine, Syria and Turkey, Macedonia and Serbia and recently the United States of America and Mexico. During the twentieth century the Berlin Wall became a symbol of the division of ideologies and perpetuated notions of enmity by focusing upon the difference between the east and west, having apparently forgotten that Germany was previously one nation, a state to which it has returned since the wall came down in 1989.

The division of people not only results in conflicts across nations but can also be the cause of personal disquiet as individuals attempt to adjust to new identities. An author of short stories who I greatly admire is Saadat Hassan Manto, a writer of genius who was committed to portraying the lives of the humble and dispossessed, many of whom lived in the poorer areas of Bombay (Mumbai). Having been brought up in the Ludhiana district of the Punjab in an Urdu speaking Muslim family, Manto was committed to the literary and cultural life of India in the years leading up to independence. In 1948 life changed for this fine writer who found it necessary to move as a muhajir with his family to the new state of Pakistan following partition, an issue that is discussed in many of his finest works. Before Manto died in 1955 he was awarded a number of national honours including the Nishan-e-Imtiaz award. We can only speculate what might have happened had partition never taken place, and Manto who was born an Indian might have died as an Indian. Perhaps he would have received similar accolades in India to those afforded by the Pakistan government.

Across the border between India and Pakistan today armed soldiers face each other, as politicians from both sides shout abuse and emphasise the differences that until 1947 were less apparent. All this following the almost arbitrary line drawn across a sub-continent by an Englishman making his one and only visit to the area. In the intervening years India and Pakistan have been to war with each other, Pakistan has itself become divided with the creation of Bangladesh, and sabres continue to be rattled across Kashmir. The differences, which are today negatively emphasised, were in the past accommodated and even celebrated.

Why should any of this matter to someone sitting in his study many thousands of miles away from India and Pakistan? I suppose it might matter a little less were it not for the fact that I have spent a great deal of my time working with colleagues in India and travelling through that beautiful country over the past twenty-five years. At the same time I have worked with university students from both India and Pakistan who have collaborated for their studies and in some instances become lifelong friends. It does matter however, because of the sadness that I feel when I see a world that is becoming ever more divided and hear the jingoistic statements made by politicians and others in authority that emphasise differences, without making an effort to understand how similar people across the world are. The major needs of an Englishman are no different from those of an Indian, a Chinaman, a Jamaican or person of any other nationality, yet it suits the purpose of some nationalistic politicians to ignore this fact. Through years of imperialist rule, my national forebears asserted what they believed to be their superiority over much of the world, exploiting resources for financial gain and deploying violence and oppression to maintain authority. Such has been the approach of major world powers and acquisitive empires throughout history. The failure of these colonial bullies to recognise the great assets of a nation's people has left scars that have not fully healed to this day.

The key to overcoming the stresses and conflicts that besiege our world must surely lie in education and the development of understanding. In today's society we have many advantages that were not available to previous generations. Unlike my grandparents, I have been able to read in translation the great literature that has been created by writers from across the globe. Writers such as Naguib Mafouz, Mahasweta Devi, Umberto Eco, Chinua Achebe and Gabriel Garcia-Marquez have provided a lens through which I have been able to view other worlds. The films of Satyajit Ray, Ingmar Bergman and Sergei Eisenstein have become easy to access and exhibitions of work by great artists such as Freda Kahlo, Amrita Sher-Gil and Marc Chagall have been featured in galleries which I can visit with minimal effort. I can relax to the recorded Sufi music of Abida Parveen, Nagauta from Japan or the techno-interpretations of Mercan Dede as easily as I can to a Mozart symphony, an Elgar concerto or Beethoven string quartet. Such opportunities if taken, should surely have awakened a more profound understanding of the inter-relationship between culture and humanity and given us ever greater cause to celebrate diversity.

I like to feel that we have come some distance towards recognising that we live in a world that is better when we break down barriers. I feel a sense of pride when I watch an English cricket team today that fields English players whose grandparents came to this country from India, Pakistan, or one of the Caribbean Islands, They I believe are every bit as British as I am, even when I can trace my ancestry back to rural Gloucestershire over many generations. Sadly, I recognise that there are others who think differently from myself and have chosen to build their own defensive walls so as not to have to encounter the rich diversity that has become the British population landscape. I understand their difficulties but firmly believe that in the future they too may come to accept that there is strength in such diversity. I suspect that it is a feeling of insecurity that has led them to erect their own personal barriers, just as there has been a lack of confidence on the part of national leaders that has resulted in the drawing of borders and the erection of walls and barbed wire fences.

In 2016, when the British Prime Minister Theresa May made the fatuous statement suggesting that *"if you believe you are a citizen of the world, you are a citizen of nowhere,"* she was pandering to an audience intent on asserting a narrow nationalistic position and reinforcing the views of those who would have us return to the restrictive definitions of identity that dominated the past. The problems that beset the world today – those associated with climate change, increasing poverty and international terrorism require a global response in which we transcend borders and cooperate in an environment of mutual respect and shared understanding. It is quite right that individuals should feel proud to be British, Brazilian, Pakistani or Russian, but is equally important to recognise that we are connected by a shared humanity that provides us with opportunities to work together and learn from each other for our mutual benefit.

In writing the stories, essays and short pieces in this book I have found myself reflecting upon those similarities and differences that exist within all of our societies. As an Englishman looking from the outside into a country in which I have made many friends, I have endeavoured to write pieces that I hope may both entertain. and from to time give cause for thought. Inevitably there will be those who speak of appropriation. What right have I as an Englishman to write about the culture and people of another land? This is a valid question, but one that I would wish to be considered from two perspectives. Firstly, that the stories and essays presented have been motivated by my feelings of great respect for the people with whom I have worked and lived in the cities and villages of India from Trivandrum to Kolkata, from Chennai to Delhi. Many of these friends and colleagues have read this work and encouraged me to publish what they have seen.

Secondly, in our efforts to gain an understanding of each other we have learned to borrow much from our differing cultures and conditions. There is evidence enough of this to be seen on the streets of any English city that are fronted by food outlets from Gujarat and Kerala, Hong Kong and Rome, Istanbul and Athens providing some of the most popular cuisine eaten in this country. Further evidence exists in the Irish bars of Bombay where young people dress in American denim and trainers while eating their burgers and French fries to the sounds of western popular music. I have even attended meetings in India where I have been greeted by men wearing surely the most ridiculous and pointless fashion accessory ever devised – the common European necktie. These may seem like trivial examples of borrowing from each other's cultures but demonstrate how despite the imposition of artificial borders, ideas, arts, cuisine, fashion and friendships flourish everywhere.

I believe that the world would have missed out greatly had not Lawrence Durrell an Englishman written about Cyprus, the American Nobel Laureate Pearl Buck not created her novels located in China, the Scottish – Sierra Leonean writer Aminatta Forna not based *"The Hired Man"* in Croatia, Anita Desai not explored the challenges faced by young Indians living in the USA and D.H Lawrence provided great insights through his essays on Mexico. What is common to each of these writers is the curiosity that they demonstrate while exploring outside of their own countries, and the appreciation that they show in portraying the people who they encounter along the way. Literature provides us with a unique opportunity to gain insights into differing interpretations of the world and must rise above the colloquial in order that we may all share in greater understanding.

Kalapurum, the location for the series of short stories in this volume does not exist. It is an amalgam of places visited, where I have been made welcome over many years. Similarly, the Sudev family and other characters portrayed are creations of my imagination and bear no intended resemblance to specific individuals. The opinions expressed in the essays and shorter pieces in this book are entirely my own. I am grateful to my many Indian friends and colleagues who have encouraged me to produce this work and to whom I dedicate it with many thanks and great affection.

Contents

Part 1

KALAPURUM FABLES

SHORT STORIES

Anil's Reward

Darkness had descended on Kalapurum and Anil was tired. It had been a long day and his labours had brought him little reward. Whilst for most of the time he enjoyed life as an auto-rickshaw driver, meeting people and showing off his skills in negotiating the teeming roads, the income to be gained was unpredictable and this had not been a good day. Such days left him feeling low and now that the early evening rush had passed, there were fewer potential passengers looking for a ride. Resigning himself to another thankless day, Anil decided to return home and hope that tomorrow's fortunes would prove better. If he hurried he might just get there before his children Bibin and Manju went to bed. He had left behind him a silent house that morning just as dawn shook the sleep from its eyes and he knew that it would feel good to be with his family tonight.

The decision having been made, with one sharp pull Anil started the engine of his auto and braced himself to join the heavy stream of vehicles vying for space and making slow progress towards the centre of Kalapurum. If the traffic continued to move at this pace with luck he might be home in less than half an hour. But if he delayed any longer the roads would be choked and he knew that with every passing minute his mood would grow darker. Yes, he thought, best to put this day behind me, go home, get some rest and look to tomorrow in hope of a better one. With this thought in mind he hoped to make good time along the potholed lanes and through the seething mass of machines which crammed the roads belching their noxious fumes.

Revving the throttle of his auto and satisfied that he had made the correct decision, Anil had travelled less than fifty yards when without warning he was confronted by a figure stepping into the road immediately in his path without any apparent regard for his own safety. His initial reaction was to make an attempt to weave around this unforeseen obstacle, but with no space in which to manoeuvre he realised the impossibility of this situation and brought his machine to an abrupt halt. Having been forced into this action, which simply added to the stresses of a day that had given him more than enough vexation, Anil glared through his windscreen and released an anguished curse.

"Bloody fool, I could have killed you!"

Staring in disbelief at the source of his angst, Anil's annoyance was intensified as this subject of his wrath now scuttled to the side of his auto and leant manically into his cabin shouting in an incomprehensible language and frantically waving a small card in his face.

Enraged by the crazed behaviour of this assailant, Anil's immediate inclination was to ignore the unwelcome infiltrator, turn the auto away from his path and make for the middle of the road. But the stranger, imposing himself in a frenzy of gesticulation and shouting, made it clear that he was not to be deterred and clung to the side of the vehicle with no apparent regard for the obvious dangers that he posed to himself, to Anil or for others who were by now weaving their way around this troublesome scene with blaring horns. Anil waved furiously in the man's face, shook his head and tried to make clear that he was not available to transport this unwelcome assailant or for that matter, any other passenger.

"Ille, ille!" he shouted in Tamil, then in hope of ensuring greater understanding in English yelled directly at the man, "No, no, I am not taking. Go away."

Being so assertive would normally have caused the most determined of would be passengers to desist, but all of this was done to no avail, as the source of his irritation persisted to cling fast to the vehicle, causing the auto to shake and roll on the road. And as the foreigner, who Anil now believed must surely be mad, shouted still louder in a language that was meaningless to the driver, the driver's exasperation and confusion intensified.

Who is this madman Anil wondered? Why has he singled me out for this attention? This had not been a good day and he feared it may be destined to become even worse. He had dealt with difficult passengers many times before. He knew from experience that sometimes angry words can quickly escalate to violence, and recognised that there might be times when he needed all his skills of reasoning to calm such situations. This man was clearly not intent on backing down or going away and Anil would need to use his many years of experience, in order to decide his next move in managing this demanding scene. He was not an unreasonable man and felt that surely he would be able to make his situation known. This bizarre event had already cost him time and he needed to make clear the urgency of his homeward journey. Hoping that this stranger might recognise his change of demeanour Anil smiled at him, shrugged his shoulders and shook his head. And indeed at this point the man did appear to lessen his wild gesticulations and seemed as if he might be prepared to listen to reason. This lessening of tensions initially appeared to have some positive effect, as the would-be passenger spoke again, but this time in much softer tones, though still in a language unrecognisable to his listener.

Looking intently at the man Anil tried to understand who this crazy character might be and why he was so persistent in his demands. Most pedestrians when rejected by an auto driver shrug their shoulders and are quickly reconciled to the fact that they will need to look elsewhere for a ride. They might curse under their breath and it was not unusual for a rejected pedestrian to release an oath in the direction of the driver or make a rude gesture, but this was something different. Clearly this man wasn't of the common sort, or he would have walked away much earlier in this encounter.

Anil's assailant was tall, sallow skinned but with dark hair creeping untidily from beneath a broad brimmed straw hat. His crumpled cream coloured suit, mud stained canvas shoes and sweat soaked shirt, worn with the top three buttons undone indicated a possible European identity, a man uncomfortable in the local climate. Yes, European thought Anil, though not British as he would most certainly have recognised at least a few words of English during their exchange. This man is, thought Anil, most likely a tourist from one of the nearby coastal resorts. If so then he will have come to Kalapurum for the same reason as all tourists to this town, to visit the Moolanathar temple with its high gopuram and great Nandi bull near to the fruit market. If this was the case then he must have been wandering around for some time as he was now two miles from this ancient site. Possibly, thought Anil, this man is now lost and this might account for his panic. But if this was the case, there were plenty of others around who could give him directions. Surely he would find someone other than himself to give him assistance.

The sweat on the man's face and that staining his far from pristine clothing, coupled with the pained expression in his eyes indicated to Anil a man who could well be in some kind of trouble, and trouble was something he didn't need at this point in the day. Anil quickly turned matters over in his mind. If the man was in trouble, then perhaps this was reason enough to make an effort to find out what the problem was and to try to offer help. After all, he wouldn't want it said that he failed to assist a stranger who was in need. But what if by providing assistance he himself ended up in difficulties, then what might be the consequences? He knew nothing of this foreigner save that his behaviour could easily be interpreted as that of a madman. Perhaps the man had been drinking, though he could smell nothing on his breath, or worse still maybe he was high on drugs. As these thoughts went through Anil's mind his anxieties intensified. Anil wasn't sure which way he should turn. Tamsi had often accused him of being indecisive, and here was surely an example of what she meant. No, not this time, he told himself, I must make my decision and stick to it. This time I will be firm.

Having pondered this situation enough, Anil's mind was made up. Once more shaking his head and indicating quite clearly that he was about to leave by pointing to the road ahead, he determined that he would recommence his irritatingly delayed journey home. Surely he thought, this will be an end to the matter. He was sorry if the man was in some kind of trouble, but it wasn't his responsibility to sort out the problems of every passing foreigner that crossed his path. And when that foreigner displayed all the symptoms of madness, this was even more reason to abandon the situation.

For what he believed would be the final time this evening Anil revved his engine and turned towards the stream of traffic. Yet if he thought to put an end to this confusing scenario he was swiftly disabused. Having appeared to have calmed greatly since his earlier outburst, the stranger now resumed his manic behaviour and became more disturbed than ever. As Anil commenced to drive away from this troublesome scene, this persistent and anguished man flung himself against the front of the auto, his face flattening full against the glass windscreen, before sliding to the road and assuming a pose akin to a supplicant praying at an altar.

This was becoming an embarrassment. Anil's resolve was wavering. Looking around he could see that this strange encounter had attracted a small audience, some of whom were pointing in his direction and laughing or shaking their heads. The plans he had made for decisive action were swiftly coming unravelled. He knew exactly what his wife would be saying to him now, he was confirming Tamsi's assertions that too often he dithered. He stared hard at the foreigner and tried to push these thoughts far back in his mind. Having initially greeted this intruder with a display of petulance, he now recognised a strategy that had been from the outset doomed to fail. Anil sighed deeply and began to mellow a little. Maybe this man really is in trouble. Perhaps this was to be his fate. Perhaps after all it was his responsibility to help a stranger in need.

The desperate man was once again clinging to his auto, pleading in words that Anil could not understand and displaying the card in his hand. Anil knew it was useless to try and understand what the foreigner was saying. Since the man had resumed his position beside the auto he had listened in an effort to discern any clue about what he was trying so desperately to communicate, but it was no use.

"Bitte, bitte, bitte hilf mir" the stranger pleaded, but his words were meaningless to the auto driver.

The words were strange and the accent strong and in his obvious anxiety to make his needs known he spoke so quickly that even if Anil had been in possession of a little of the language he would have struggled to pick up more than the occasional word.

Why me? Anil asked himself. There are other auto drivers around this area, so why am I the chosen one? Why else would he have stopped Anil in his auto other than to seek a ride? Could there be another motive? But then when he could see his reluctance to accept his fare he should surely have looked to another driver. So much was obvious, but the panic that was evident in this man's eyes made him wary of giving in to his pleading. Perhaps, thought Anil, beginning to feel some sympathy, he may want to travel in the direction of my home. This being the case I could take him as the last fare of the day. Yes, this would be a fair compromise. I should have thought of this before, it would have saved so much time. But before he would let him aboard his auto he needed confirmation of the destination required by this ardent would be passenger who continued to assail him with his incomprehensible speech.

Remembering the card which had been waved in his face Anil gestured towards the man, who quickly understood that Anil was prepared to consider the urgency of his demands. Taking one hand from the frame of the auto and pushing this into the pocket of his jacket he produced the card and handed it to the driver who scanned it before looking back to the stranger and shaking his head. Coconut Grove Beach Resort, the address clearly displayed on the card in English on one side and Tamil on the other, was two miles in the opposite direction to Anil's home. Now he knew that he should have been much firmer when he had the chance. If he took this passenger to his required destination it would be at least an hour before he would be home. By that time he would be too late to see his children before they went to bed and all for the sake of a fifty rupee fare.

Shaking his head Anil made what he hoped would be correctly interpreted as placatory noises and pointed in the direction of his home, hoping the man would finally understand and let him leave. Once again he resolved to turn his auto-rickshaw into the traffic, he had wasted enough time with this strange man and now just wanted to make his way back to his family. But just as before, the deranged fellow stepped out ahead of him with seemingly no regard for his safety causing Anil to hit his brakes and arrest his progress. Anil let out a scream, cursing this lunatic and deciding that far more drastic action was now needed. He would get out of his auto and push this infuriating man to the side of the road. He would use minimal force but would assert his right to be left alone. With increased determination he began to leave his cab, now committed to the action that he would take and which would bring an end to this nonsense. Poised for action, with one foot on the road and about to make his first contact with the foreigner, his movement was suddenly arrested when he noticed another piece of paper being waved in his direction by the intended target of his anger.

Could this be what it seemed? The man brought his hand closer to Anil's face continuing to wield what could now be clearly recognised as a five hundred rupee note. Anil hesitated; was this some kind of trick? What could this mean? Who would pay 500 rupees for a two mile ride in an auto-rickshaw? Did this simply confirm the madness of this stranger? Now he was unsure what he should do. His earlier resolve was fast dissolving. If this strange man was seriously offering him ten times the standard fare, then how could he refuse? Five hundred rupees was a lot of money, almost as much as he had managed to make during a whole day of working. Was this man serious about paying so much?

As Anil's mind raced through his options the man drew nearer and before he realised what was happening the 500 rupee note had been pushed into the top pocket of his khaki jacket and the stranger had leapt into the vehicle and positioned himself on the seat behind him. Anil turned and stared hard at the man, but could immediately see how he had braced himself against the sides of the vehicle and was firmly planted in the seat. Now he is actually inside the auto, thought Anil, it will be almost impossible to move him without a struggle. If he was seen wrestling with a foreigner he could find himself in trouble with the police. What could he do? It appeared that a decision had been made for him, though Anil was unsure how. The stranger had taken control and there was little that Anil could do about the situation. But the 500 rupee note now safely in his pocket had changed the circumstances of this event and sealed the fate of both himself and his passenger; for passenger was what the foreigner had surely now become. This action of the foreigner brought a significant change to the course of the evening. Anil shook his head, but acknowledging an opportunity to bring this evening's charade to a conclusion as quickly as possible, turned in the opposite direction to his home and nosed his auto across the busy lanes of traffic.

With any luck Anil knew, they could reach the coast road within the next fifteen minutes and generally from there the journey to Coconut Grove would be straightforward. With this in mind and having decided to make the best of this bizarre situation Anil threaded his way between cars, trucks, two wheelers and the occasional cyclist in the hope that this would be the busiest part of the route. At first the progress made was good and Anil believed that his hopes might be realised, but then for reasons unknown, as is often the case on the roads of Kalapurum, for no one as yet has managed to understand the traffic in India; all vehicles came to a standstill. As is the custom in such situations in Kalapurum, as elsewhere across the country, drivers used their horns unsparingly in a forlorn belief that this might somehow cause the traffic to once more flow. But Anil had experienced this congestion a thousand times before and resigned himself to switching off his engine to conserve fuel and wait until movement recommenced.

Leaning forward from his seat Anil's passenger tapped him sharply on the shoulder and pointing at the watch on his wrist spoke again with words, that whilst quite alien to Anil's ear could be easily interpreted as conveying a heightened level of anxiety. Anil shrugged and pointed at the vehicles lined across the road in front of him indicating that there was nothing he could do, at which point the foreigner let out a loud cry and settled back heavily into his seat, his face betraying resignation and despondency. By now Anil, having committed himself to this journey felt more than a little sympathy for his charge. His passenger was clearly desperate and having accepted his money he felt obliged to do the best he could to reach his destination as quickly as might safely be managed. Whatever the outcome of this mission, he would not have it said that he did anything less than his best to get this stranger to his desired terminus. Furthermore, the 500 rupee note in his pocket helped to ease the pain of knowing that yet again he would miss seeing Bibin and Manju when he eventually reached home.

At last movement was detected ahead and Anil, having restarted his engine began to inch forward into the congestion. Feeling a renewed commitment to his distraught passenger he eased his way through the smallest spaces, ignoring the oaths and gestures of drivers around him and with gaining confidence made his way in the direction of the coast road. The usual bellowing of horns signified the determination of all around to keep progressing towards their final destinations and thankfully the chaotic traffic kept moving. Within another ten minutes his first objective had been reached and as Anil manoeuvred his way onto the broad highway he could believe that this fraught evening would soon be at an end. As he accelerated away, his attention was once again gained by the man in the rear of his auto tapping him on the shoulder. Looking around and fearing the worst, Anil was greeted this time with a smile as the man said something, which he interpreted as being an affirmation of his efforts to get him to his objective as quickly as possible. This calmer demeanour from his passenger was greatly welcomed and brought Anil some relief.

The final mile of the journey to the Coconut Grove Beach Resort, much to Anil's relief, passed without further incident. Reaching their destination and pulling across the road Anil halted at the gateway that marked the entrance to the resort, where the duty watchman checked the vehicle prior to opening a barrier and waving them through. Within a hundred yards of passing through the gate they arrived at an open area in front of the resort's reception building and before Anil had fully come to a stop his passenger sprang from the auto and was hurtling in the direction of a taxi parked near the door. Under normal circumstances the driver would have been amazed and possibly even alarmed by the stranger's unusual behaviour, but having some time ago reached the conclusion that this man was in some way deranged, he simply shrugged his shoulders. What had been the source of this man's desperation, wondered Anil? Whatever it might be, having come this far he was determined to see the conclusion to this strange evening's events and remained seated in his auto reviewing the scene before him.

Within twenty strides of escaping the auto Anil's passenger had reached the taxi, just as the driver had started its engine and appeared to be ready for departure. With an action reminiscent of those witnessed earlier in the evening, the man without hesitation threw himself in front of the departing vehicle half sprawling across the taxi's bonnet whilst simultaneously omitting a loud scream. This crazed gesture hardly surprised Anil, who in truth expected nothing less than a continuation of the madness with which he had come to associate his former passenger. This latest assault from the foreigner had what Anil could only imagine to have been the desired effect of bringing the taxi to a grinding halt. At this point the man, whom Anil had come to think of as the insane protagonist at the centre of a persistent nightmare, slid from the bonnet and raced to the side of the taxi. Here, with one swift movement he pulled open a rear door of the car. By now Anil believed that there would be nothing in this foreigner's behaviour that would surprise him and he expected the persistent man to leap into the cab much as he had into his own more modest vehicle earlier in the evening. But this was not to be, and he was taken aback when rather than entering the taxi the man leaned forward into the cab and took by the hand an elegantly dressed Indian woman who stepped from within to join him beside the vehicle. Immediately on leaving the cab this latest performer in the drama flung herself into the arms the auto driver's former passenger. Anil could do no more than stare as for fully two minutes these two main players in this confusing scene clung to each other in a firm embrace. Who, he asked himself, can this odd couple be? She dressed so magnificently in a stunning maroon and gold sari, with fine jewels, a jasmine garland arranged delicately in her hair and golden sandals on her tiny feet, and he by contrast in such a dishevelled state. It seems, he thought, that I may have delivered my passenger here just in time. This beautiful young woman was obviously about to leave, but why and where to? What might the situation have been had I arrived ten minutes later? Anil once more shook his head, still confused by the scene he was witnessing as the taxi driver unloaded two heavy cases from the boot of his car.

Perhaps the evening had reached a satisfactory conclusion. After all, thought Anil with a wry smile. After all I never doubted that the right thing to do was to take my passenger to his destination, as is the duty of any good auto-rickshaw driver. For the final time this evening he started his engine ready to make his way homeward, but as he was about to head back to the road he noticed the man and the women beckoning to him to stop. Anil hesitated, by now he had endured enough excitement for one evening and his inclination was to ignore this command and make a speedy departure. Walking hand in hand towards him, she with tears running down her cheeks, and his former passenger smiling broadly they drew near and Anil decided that perhaps it would be better to wait and see what might now transpire.

"Nandri, rombo nandri", cried the woman, the first expression he had heard in his own language since the confusing events of the evening had begun. His former passenger lifted his hat, smiled and uttered one final incomprehensible sentence. "Danke dir. Danke. Vielen dank für ihre freundlichkeit". Anil smiled, waved and moved off, determined not to look back as he drove away from Coconut Grove Resort towards the coast road and home.

Having checked once more that the 500 rupee note was safely located in his pocket Anil knew that he had understood very little of what had passed before him this evening. Once more turning his auto into the streaming traffic, he headed home and laughed.

The Elephant Brooch

"I was named after the Nightingale of India, the great poet Sarojini Naidu", said Paati. "You see my parents were both members of the Congress and workers for the freedom of India. Of course, I was just a small child and it wasn't until much later that I came to know the significance of my name. I was ten years old when Sarojini Naidu passed away and when I read about what she had achieved I felt so proud to be the bearer of her name".

Bibin and Manju loved to hear the stories that their great grandmother told from her youth. Life when she was young must have been so much different from that which they experienced today and although they had heard most of Paati's tales many times, they never tired of this repetition. Paati was old, but her memory was good and her attention to detail held the attention of her great grandchildren, much as had been the case for their parents and grandparents in earlier years. She had been born during a defining period of Indian history and it was not only her family that knew the importance of the momentous events that she recalled.

Today was Paati's 78th Birthday and as is invariably the situation when children spend time with those from earlier generations, in the eyes of Bibin and Manju she appeared very old. Although they saw their great grandmother almost every day, today was special and the two children came bearing gifts to celebrate such an auspicious occasion. Paati had a sweet tooth and knowing this, Talsi had taken her children by bus to Chennai to purchase gifts from the Sri Krishna sweet shop in Anna Nagar. Whilst the colourful displays and delicious aromas of the shop could have justified a lengthy stay at this delectable store, their visit was in fact quite brief. Everyone in the Sudev family knew that what Paati loved best were the rich mysurpa and kesar peda, which had been such a treat in childhood and it was with a box of each of these delicacies that they had returned to Kalapurum yesterday afternoon.

Bibin and Manju had chosen colourful paper in which to wrap their gifts and it was with great pleasure, and perhaps a little anticipation that Paati would want to share the contents of the boxes, that they watched her peel the wrapping from these presents. The smile that lit up their grandmother's face was enough to confirm her delight as the boxes were revealed. Taking each child in turn Paati hugged them close to her breast, thanking them for the wisdom of the choice of sweets that they had made, whilst surreptitiously offering Talsi a knowing and grateful smile. And just as Bibin and Manju had hoped, within minutes along with Paati and their mother, they were savouring the sweet contents of the boxes.

Birthdays are generally happy occasions, but they can also be a time for reminiscence and sometimes for sad memories. It is often small details or occurrences that provoke such recollections, as was the case today as Paati enjoyed the company of her close knit family. It was amidst all of the family banter and laughter that Manju first noticed the silver brooch shaped like an elephant that was catching the sunlight from where it was pinned on the breast of Paati's sari. She was sure that she had seen it before, but equally confident that it was not an ornament worn by her grandmother often. Indeed, apart from her earrings and on special occasions a gold necklace, Paati seldom wore jewellery of any description.

"Paati," began Manju, "that is such a beautiful brooch that you are wearing. Have you had it since you were young?"

Paati raised her right hand to her breast, stroking the brooch and looking down as if to remind herself of its detail. For a while she was quiet and Manju could see that her grandmother was thinking before making a response, but eventually she looked up at Manju, and then at Bibin and smiled.

"Yes indeed, I can tell you the exact date on which I was given this beautiful brooch," she said with a sigh. "I wear it on special occasions because it brings me many happy memories, but I don't wear it often because it can also make me sad." With this seemingly contradictory expression Paati unpinned the brooch from her sari and handed it carefully to Manju who examined it closely, turning it over in her hand. Bibin, whose interest in this obviously significant bijou had been aroused as much as his sister's, reached out his hand and Manju gently passed it to him feeling that this might indeed be a precious jewel.

Watching the care with which the children handled the brooch, Paati offered words of reassurance. "You are not likely to harm it you know. It is not worth a lot of money; although it is silver in colour it is made of a much less valuable metal. None the less, it means a great deal to me and is one of my most treasured possessions. If you look carefully you will see a small hole where once the elephant had a shiny green glass eye. Sadly the eye must have fallen out several years ago and now it is lost. Otherwise the brooch is exactly as it was when it was given to me all those years ago."

"Was it a birthday present?" asked Bibin. "Who gave it to you?"

"No," replied Paati, "not a birthday present, but still something which at the time meant much to me, and continues to be one of my most precious treasures, even after so many years."

Manju's curiosity had been raised to such a pitch that she was desperate to know more about the elephant shaped object that Bibin had now returned to her care. "Will you tell us more about who gave it to you Paati, was it a gift from Tâttâ?"

"Oh, no," Paati exclaimed. "I was given this before I ever met my dear husband." Paati looked at the inquisitive faces of her great grandchildren and knew that they would not be satisfied until she had told them the whole story behind the elephant brooch. "I will tell you," she said, "but you must remember that the story concerns things that happened a long time ago. Things that at the time I was too young to understand; in fact things that I still don't fully understand today. I was only a child, younger even than you are now Manju. When I was given this precious gift I was just eight years old."

Paati sighed and shook her head and Manju could see that she was delving into her memories and sensed that these might not all be as happy as she would wish on this important day of celebration. "It's ok Paati," she exclaimed. "If you don't want to tell the story, it doesn't matter."

Paati smiled. "It's fine, the story needs to be told. It is part of our family history and I hope that one day, when you have children of your own who are old enough, you might also tell it to them." Manju and Bibin remained silent, they sensed that it was important now to let Paati continue her story without interruption. Paati recognised the anticipation in their faces and determined that having raised their expectations she would carry on.

"I think you already know," she began, "that when I was a very small child for a while I lived with my parents in Delhi. We had a home near Sadar Bazaar where my father was selling Khadi cloth; I told you that my parents were committed to the freedom movement, and this was a way in which they could make a contribution to that cause. It was a busy district very crowded with people from all over India, there was always something happening and I loved living there. I had many friends when I was young, but the best of all was Saadia who like me was not originally from Delhi, her parents having come to the city from a village in the Punjab. Saadia and I went everywhere together; we were the best of friends and were in and out of each other's houses and getting into all kinds of mischief." Paati laughed and shook her head, "such wonderful times, so many happy memories." She is quiet for a moment before continuing.

"Just like all children I suppose, Saadia and I had many dreams. We spent so much time talking about what we would do in the future, promising to always be friends. But sadly not all of the dreams that we have can come true, and not all of the plans that we make are bound to happen. This is something I learned in Delhi, and it was a hard lesson that I have never forgotten. You see it was Saadia who gave me the lovely elephant brooch that you are cradling in your hand. I remember the day very clearly. Indeed I think of the occasion often and see Saadia's face as if it were just yesterday." As she listened to her grandmother Manju noticed that her eyes had begun to water. She wondered if she should say something, perhaps to break the reverie that was clearly causing her great grandmother discomfort, but before she could decide what actions she might take Paati continued."

"For several weeks I knew there had been trouble. My father forbade me to go alone around the streets and as soon as darkness fell I was confined to the house. I wasn't sure what was happening, but I heard adults talking in hushed voices and I could see that some were preparing to make journeys. For more than a week I had not seen Saadia and knew that something must be wrong. I asked my mother but she told me not to worry, that she had seen Saadia's mother and that the family were making preparations for a journey, probably to return to their village in the Punjab. I found this difficult to understand. Saadia had told me nothing of a planned visit to her village. How long I wondered, would she be gone? Surely as her best friend I would have known if this were going to happen. I could sense that something was causing people to be frightened, but nobody would tell me what it was. My parents kept reassuring me that all would be well and I had nothing to worry about. But when you are a small child and nothing in the world makes sense, it is not always easy to accept reassurance, even from those who are closest to you."

"Then one day, I remember it well, it was a Monday morning, Saadia arrived at our door. I was overjoyed to see her and clasped her closely to my breast. I could sense that she too was pleased that we were back together, but then I looked at her face and saw tears tumbling down her cheeks. I couldn't understand. Why I asked was she crying, was she not happy to see me? Now that she had returned wouldn't everything be just as it was before? But I could tell. I knew just by looking at Saadia's eyes that all was not going to be as it had been. She struggled to speak, but between sobs told me that the time had come for her family to leave Delhi, that they must travel back to their village in the Punjab and that her father told her to come quickly to say goodbye as we were never likely to see each other again."

"Of course I thought this was a mistake. We were such close friends; we were bound to meet again. I tried to be assertive. When I am old enough, I told Saadia, I will come and find you and we will be together again. But Saadia simply shook her head and turned to leave, and as she did so she pushed a small cloth bound package into my hand. She reached up, stroked my hair then turned and was gone before I could say anything more. I started to run after her, but my mother who had been watching from the doorway stopped me. I was angry and confused, but my mother held me tight and told me that I must stay home and I must let Saadia go."

Paati's eyes were now filled with tears and Manju was anxious that she might have inadvertently been the cause of her distress. She reached out for Paati's hand and said, "I'm sorry Paati, I didn't want to make you to be sad on your birthday."

Patti wiped away her tears and smiled at Manju. "You have not made me sad Manju, it is a story that needs to be told so that none of us can forget."

"So Patti," it was now Bibin who spoke. "Was it the elephant brooch wrapped in the cloth?"

"Yes, that's right," answered Paati. "It was my beautiful precious elephant brooch. I will never forget that day, it was Monday September 22nd 1947, the last time I saw Saadia, the day she gave me the elephant brooch with the green glass eye."

"And you never saw her after that day?" asked Manju.

"No, not ever again. All I know is that she left Delhi on a train. At the time when she left I knew nothing of the terrible journeys that Muslims were forced to make to the new country of Pakistan, or about the terrible fate of Hindus coming south. Thousands arrived in Delhi over the next few weeks. Today we know too much of the dreadful things that happened." Once again Paati fell silent and Manju found herself also lost for words.

"I like to think," said Paati as she regained some composure. "That somewhere in what is now Pakistan, my dear friend Saadia, just like me enjoys birthday celebrations with her family, perhaps with great grandchildren just like you. I dream that she sits with them and tells them tales and remembers our happy days in Old Delhi, and that she smiles and knows that here in India I too recall those wonderful times together. And that you see is why my elephant brooch is the most precious piece of jewellery that I own, and why I will always wear it on my birthday to bring back memories, both happy and sad.

The Missing Hero

1.

For Bibin, as for many other Indian boys and girls in Kalapurum, cricket was a passion. Some would even say that it had surpassed all normal levels of enthusiasm and had graduated to become an obsession. Before and after school and at weekends Bibin, in company with as many friends as he could muster, would hurry to Sethupathi Park where makeshift stumps fashioned from three ill-matched lengths of bamboo, a crudely carved bat and a balding tennis ball provided all the equipment needed to secure a game that could last for many hours.

Bibin's sister Manju did not share her brother's interest in cricket or any other games, but there was one aspect of his enthusiasm that she observed with quiet admiration, though she would never have admitted this to him. Manju was a studious girl, who preferred to spend her time immersed in a book or writing poetry, but she held her brother in some regard for the knowledge that he had accumulated about the game he loved and those who played it. Much of the information he had gained, and which he would willingly share with anyone inclined to listen to endless lists of facts and statistics, had been obtained from the colourful cards depicting India's cricketing heroes of the past and today, which could be purchased in packs of five from the local corner grocery.

In the midst of any conversation, which might be about any subject other than cricket, Bibin was likely to share with great authority a raft of facts from his vast cornucopia of cricketing trivia. Examples of these occasions were aplenty, such as the time one morning at breakfast when he suddenly announced, apropos nothing in particular, "Do you know that Anil Kumble took 619 test match wickets, more than any other Indian player, and that he once took all ten Pakistan wickets in an innings? Isn't that incredible?" Those seated around the table, having become accustomed to such declarations nodded silently and feigned a little interest, but devoted marginally less attention to Bibin's supposedly interesting facts than was currently demanded by the idli and sambar on plates before them.

While Manju had not the least interest in the statistics associated with cricket, and indeed had only a vague notion of a cricketer named Kumble, she did hold a quiet admiration for her brother's ability to learn and retain such figures. Maybe, she thought, if Bibin's teachers taught all his mathematics through the medium of cricket, he might prove to be a genius.

Some of the cards that had been collected by Bibin were strategically arranged on the wall beside his bed, in the room that he shared with Manju. A dividing curtain strung across the centre of their room provided demarcation of their individual territory, and a visitor to this space would be in no doubt as to which sibling occupied each given half. Manju's space could best be described as pristine, with books neatly arranged along a makeshift bookcase comprising four wooden shelves hewn from an old packing case and supported on bricks. On the wall beside her neatly arranged bed, two framed pictures, one of Gandhi working at a charka and one taken from an old calendar depicting a scene from the Himalaya formed the only decoration in her half of the room. Her clothes neatly ordered and folded, were carefully arranged on a chair beside her bed. By contrast, Bibin's quarters were strewn with much of the paraphernalia associated with his passion. A pile of well-thumbed Cricket Today magazines, and cuttings from the Deccan Herald reporting the performances of local, state and national teams, littered both the floor and Bibin's unkempt bed. Crumpled clothing, bags of ill-defined detritus and discarded sweet wrappers littered the floor. Leaning against the wall, his prized possession, a much worn and taped cricket bat gifted to him by an uncle, far too large for him to manage at present, but with which he intended to score many boundaries in the future, took pride of place and acted as a stimulus for many of Bibin's finest aspirations.

It was however, the card collection which adorned the wall that stood out in his half of the room. Not only for the colourful display which they made against a grey plastered background, but more especially for the orderly fashion in which they were arranged. Here was a considerable contrast with the apparent chaos that dominated much of Bibin's domain. Each card was neatly ordered beneath a hand drawn banner proclaiming "India's Greatest Players". In this reverential display each sportsman had been positioned only after careful contemplation of where they should be located in a distinct pecking order, based upon their achievements with bat and ball, but more especially upon the impact they had on Bibin's imagination.

Portrayed on this wall could be seen many of the great performers of today, Virat Kohli, Rohit Sharma, Ravindra Jadeja and M.S Dohni each depicted in action with bat or ball and accompanied by details of their best performances and records in tests and limited overs games. In amongst these modern gladiators were other great players from the past, Sunil Gavaskar, Mohamed Azarudeen, Kapil Dev, Bishen Bedi and Anil Kumble similarly posed and carefully pasted to Bibin's handmade chart. One glance at this exhibition was enough to demonstrate the pride which Bibin took in the collection and his dedication to the sport.

Bibin could often be found seated on his bed, considering his display and shuffling through a pile of cards illustrating players, who had not quite met his criteria for a place upon the wall of honour that he had created. He had often wondered about Virender Sehwag and Harbhajan Singh, neither of whom had quite made it to the wall. Was he perhaps underestimating their contribution to the game? The records of some of the great players of the past represented on his cards, the Newab of Pataudi, Mohinder Amarnath and Vijay Hazare would most certainly justify their inclusion, but perhaps because they came from a distant age and had not attracted Bibin's immediate attention, they hadn't made the cut.

Such dilemmas far from troubling Bibin provided him many happy hours of diversion, and often served as a useful means of displacement activity when he should have been focused upon his homework. However, on too many occasions as he lay upon his bed gazing at the display that he had made, his attention was drawn to an empty space, one that awaited the arrival of the player who he knew should be located at the summit of the pyramid of greatness that he had built, but who had thus far eluded him.

Every Saturday morning for the past six months on receiving the small sum of pocket money given to him by his father for the menial chores that he conducted during the week, Bibin had dashed to the corner shop to purchase a pack of five cards. On leaving the shop he would eagerly tear open the packaging to reveal the colourful pictures inside, sorting through them in the hope that this week his missing hero would be amongst them. Throughout these months the same pattern had been followed with a similar disappointing result. Yet another Dhoni, a fourth Yuvraj Singh, and a fifth Dilip Vengsarkar, but never the elusive master of them all; never Sachin Tendulkar. Returning home Bibin would add the latest acquisitions to his growing pile of cards and curse the unfairness of a situation in which at least four of his friends had bought packets containing Tendulkar, whilst he had never hit this long-awaited jackpot. One of his classmates had to his knowledge at one time held three Tendulkar cards in his possession but had swapped these with other students before Bibin had a chance to negotiate.

At first Bibin had thought that it would only be a matter of time before his luck would change. But as time had passed and each week his precious pocket money had bought him nothing more than duplicates of cards already in his collection, he began to despair. Before long Manju and his parents found themselves hardly daring to ask for news as Bibin returned from his Saturday shopping excursion. The name of Sachin Tendulkar was never mentioned in Bibin's presence and even during his absence was spoken only in hushed tones. Hardly daring to broach the subject, Manju and her parents quietly hoped that before too long the Little Maestro as Tendulkar was often named, would put in an appearance and relieve them of the tension which surrounded their Saturday mornings.

2.

As with Bibin, every Saturday Morning Manju would collect a few rupees from her father in lieu of small jobs performed during the week. Unlike Bibin, Manju was more inclined to save her earnings until she had identified a potential purchase that she regarded as justifying parting with her money. In recent weeks Mr Desai the principal of Manju and Bibin's school had taken to reading a story to the assembled students as the last act of Friday afternoons, before dismissing his charges for the weekend. Manju who for some time had been in love with literature, found herself transfixed as each week's story painted pictures in her imagination. Most recently the principal's readings had been taken from a collection of tales written by that great master of storytelling R.K Narayan. These had so enchanted and amused Manju, who had determined that she would save her pocket money until she would have accrued sufficient funds to visit Katha Bookshop and buy a copy of Malgudi Days, which Mr Desai had suggested she would greatly enjoy.

Each Saturday Manju had added her pocket money to that from previous weeks and placed her accumulating wealth in a box on her bookshelves. Having visited Katha Bookshop and spoken to its owner Mr Prasad, she knew precisely how much money she needed to purchase Malgudi Days, and the kindly proprietor had ordered a copy in anticipation of Manju acquiring the required amount. It was therefore with great anticipation that on the fifth Saturday after beginning her savings, Manju realised that she had finally saved the exact total needed to make her desired purchase.

Keenly anticipating an afternoon lying on her bed and reading her newly purchased book, Manju set out purposefully towards the bookshop. Along the route she repeated in her mind the tale of Rajam and Mani most recently recited by Mr Desai and looked forward to immersing herself in the wonderful woven words that awaited her in Narayan's writing.

Half an hour later Manju entered Katha Bookshop where she observed that Mr Prasad accompanied by a customer was busily hunting amongst the crowded shelves, presumably in pursuit of a specific title. In no hurry, she began to indulge herself in a favourite pastime, that of grazing the well laden bookshelves, picking out books which may be of interest and making mental notes of titles and authors she would explore in the future. Familiar names; Ruskin Bond, Mulk Raj Anand and A.K Ramanujan sat shoulder to shoulder with those as yet unknown; Raja Rao, Shashi Deshpande and Meena Kandasamy whose books in future years Manju would come to regard as close companions. Manju moved slowly, navigating the shelves, indulging herself in the comforting smell of the books and the familiar textures of pages and dust jackets, until she came to the far end of the shop where she knew she would find a box containing volumes that had been reduced in price, possibly because of a soiled cover or torn dust jacket, or maybe because they had occupied Katha Bookshop for too long with no one interested enough to give them a new home.

In the past, Manju had on occasion turned over the books in this box in the hope of uncovering a title of interest, and indeed had twice purchased such texts at greatly reduced prices. Today, knowing that her quarry was a specific title held in waiting for her by Mr Prasad, she visited the pile of bargain books with no purpose other than that of passing time. Lifting a couple of volumes from the box with great care, for Manju quite rightly believed that books deserved to be granted respect, she idly scanned their covers, exploring illustrations, titles and authors before returning them to their place. It was during this diversionary process that she noticed in the depths of the receptacle, a plastic folder, which on further scrutiny revealed in its contents a set of familiar objects. Leaning over the box and moving to one side a large encyclopaedia and an edition of Collins Concise German Dictionary in order that she could gain better access, Manju took up the plastic folder to more closely examine its colourful contents.

Only the briefest of perusals was needed for Manju to confirm that the clear plastic folder contained a set of cards identical to those with which she was so familiar from the display in Bibin's half of their bedroom. Opening the folder, she removed and began to manipulate the cards, looking at faces and actions that she had come to recognise, though not to an extent where she could accurately name the cricketers depicted. The folder must have contained more than a hundred cards, none of which under normal circumstances would have commanded more than a fleeting glimpse from Manju. Indeed, as she turned over the cards in her hand, she became ever more convinced that cricket was never likely to fire her imagination in the manner that the hundreds of books surrounding her, most definitely could. But now, as she held these objects in her hands, the thought came to her that she just might have come across hidden treasure. Just suppose, she thought, that somewhere within this collection lies the very object of Bibin's obsession. Might it be possible, that here amongst these cards that held little interest for herself, she would find the elusive card bearing a portrait and the records of the evasive Sachin Tendulkar?

With her usual attention to detail Manju began a systematic shuffling of the cards. Here were names which through her brother, Manju despite her lack of enthusiasm for cricket, had come to recognise; Sourav Ganguly, M.S. Dhoni, V.V.S. Laxman. Ten, twenty, maybe thirty cards had been scanned when there at last, held between her fingers was a card bearing the unmistakable image of Sachin Tendulkar. Manju could never have anticipated that she would feel such excitement from discovering a card, which for her was of so little interest. Yet at this instant she was aware of a broad grin lighting up her face and the customer with whom Mr Prasad had been engaged, and was now about to leave the shop, turned to see from where the loudly uttered cry of "yes" had emerged.

Returning the card to the folder, Manju hesitated as she wondered what her next action should be. She knew that in her possession at this moment was the very item most coveted by her cricket mad brother. As she stood staring at the plastic folder her reverie was disturbed by the distinctive voice of Mr Prasad, summoning her from across the shop.

"Good morning Manju, I thought you might be in today. I have your copy of Malgudi Days here beneath the counter waiting for you."

Manju turned and acknowledged the friendly bookseller, but still held on to the plastic folder containing the many cards. Here in her hands she knew that she held the potential to bring joy to her brother and relief to the whole family. How then should she proceed? Mr Prasad had confirmed that the book, for which she had saved her hard-earned pocket money over many weeks, was awaiting her collection. In her pocket she had just the right sum of 1,200 rupees to make her purchase, but now found herself facing a dilemma and realised that she must decide. She had entered the shop clear in her mission, but now she was confused and wondering what the right thing to do would be.

Approaching the counter carrying the folder, she smiled at Mr Prasad and enquired of him;

"This folder contains a lot of cards about cricketers, if I want to buy just one card, the one with a picture of Sachin Tendulkar, would that be possible?"

"Ah, Sachin Tendulkar, always a great favourite," began Mr Prasad as he played an imaginary perfect forward defensive stroke before his customer. "Indeed, I would tend to agree with those who say he is the greatest batsman of all time, greater even than Bradman many say. Though of course the great Australian played well before my time."

Manju nodded without revealing that she was not quite sure who Bradman was, or might have been. "So, is it possible to buy just that one card?" she repeated her question.

"Oh no, I'm afraid not," replied the bookseller. "You see these are much sought after by collectors, and therefore I can only sell the folder with all of its contents. The folder contains a full set of all the cards in the collection and I am sure I will eventually have a customer who wishes to buy the whole package. If I were to remove cards, this would most certainly make the package less attractive to the ardent collector"

"And how much would the whole package cost?" Manju enquired, already feeling a sense of disappointment.

"Now let me see." The bookseller took the folder from Manju as if weighing its value in his hands. "I think I could let the collection go for 800 rupees, particularly if I knew they were going to a real enthusiast such as you seem to be."

Manju pondered the situation. A real enthusiast she thought was certainly a description that could be applied to Bibin, though most certainly not to herself. But 800 rupees, when all that was needed was a single card seemed to be excessive. As Manju considered her dilemma another customer entered the shop and Mr Prasad, with Manju's consent went to speak to the newcomer.

Opening the folder Manju once more removed the image of Tendulkar. Here she knew was the source of all Bibin's recent strife. With one purchase she believed that she could make him the happiest boy in Kalapurum. But if she were to leave this package here in the bookshop, she knew that Bibin could never save the money needed for its purchase, and even if he did, by the time he had 800 rupees, the chances were that the collection would have been bought by some other fanatic. What was she to do? As she turned the problem over in her mind she became aware that Mr Prasad had returned and knew that the time had come to bring her procrastination to a conclusion.

"Mr Prasad," she now spoke with what she hoped sounded like an element of authority, her mind having been made up. "If I were to buy this collection of cards, do you think you could keep the copy of Malgudi Days for a few more weeks? I promise that I will then return and buy the book."

Mr Prasad smiled down at Manju. "I see," he began. "I have always seen you as an avid reader and enthusiast for books, I had never imagined you to be a great cricket fan. Of course, I will be happy to keep the book under the counter until you are ready to return and buy it."

The decision having been made, Manju thanked the kindly proprietor and counted out 800 rupees which she handed to him in exchange for the folder and its contents. Even now she was uncertain whether her actions made sense. It had taken her many weeks to accumulate 1,200 rupees, and she had been looking forward all week to returning home with her much-anticipated new book. But the deed was now done, she had parted with her money and there must be no regrets. Tucking the folder beneath her arm she left the shop and commenced her journey home.

3.

Arriving at home Manju found the house deserted. Her father she knew would be working, scouring the streets looking for passengers in his auto-rickshaw, and her mother had probably gone to the market to purchase vegetables. As for Bibin, this being a Saturday he would almost certainly be found at Sethupathi Park playing cricket with a group of friends.

Having made a selfless decision to purchase a set of cards in which she had very little interest, other than that of pleasing her brother and bringing peace to the household, Manju decided that she would arrange a surprise for Bibin. Having formulated a plan, she entered the shared bedroom and removed the cards from the plastic folder. Kneeling beside Bibin's bed, she reached beneath and pulled out the cardboard shoebox in which her brother kept his prized collection. Taking the new set of cards, she began to place these into the box, mixing them randomly with others so that when Bibin next shuffled through his hoard, he might come by chance upon his missing hero. As she pictured this image in her mind she smiled and looked forward to her brother's reaction on finding Sachin Tendulkar hidden amongst the other cards. Only after his discovery and allowing him a little time of puzzlement, would Manju tell him of her deed.

Having completed her stealthy mission and feeling particularly pleased with her intrigue, Manju began to push the box back into place beneath Bibin's bed, now convinced that her decision to buy the cards had been a good one. It was only at this point that she became aware of a noise indicating someone standing behind her in the room.

"What do you think you're doing?" The question shouted by Bibin from only a few yards away startled Manju, who turned and began to raise herself up from the floor. Before she could think how to answer without revealing her secret, Bibin commenced a violent tirade.

"This is my side of the room, you have no right to be here going through my things. Your space is the other side of the curtain. I don't want you interfering with my things. Do you hear me? What are you playing at? I don't mess with your books, so you leave my things alone. If I catch you going through my property again I'll give you a good thrashing, do you hear?"

Manju had heard all too well. She was flustered and embarrassed at having been discovered behaving in such a surreptitious manner. Her intentions had been good. No, not just good, more than this, her motives had been kind. But now she was facing her brother's ire and didn't know how to respond. She could feel tears welling in her eyes, as pushing quickly past Bibin she fled from the room and didn't stop running until she reached the end of the street. There she flung herself down on a patch of grass and sat for quite some time waiting for her heart to stop racing, whilst contemplating all that had passed since leaving home earlier in the day.

4.

That evening at the family meal Manju felt uncomfortable. Not knowing whether she should tell Bibin the full story of her morning's activities or remain silent. She opted for the latter option. The image of Bibin finding the card and being overjoyed remained in her mind, though this was juxtaposed with negative feelings in respect of the injustice that she felt had fallen upon her shoulders. Pretending to be focused on the meal, which her mother had prepared, she found herself unable to lift her eyes in Bibin's direction and hoped that soon the situation would be resolved, and life might return to normal. If the meal would only pass without a recommencement of hostilities, she would be able to escape to the sanctuary of her room. Manju's mother, ever astute and sensitive to the needs of her family, could sense the unease around the table and sought to understand the causes of the tensions that were manifest between Bibin and his sister. Looking first at Bibin and then at her daughter, Talsi tried to break the ice between them with small talk.

"So then, have you both been busy today? What have you been up to?"

Manju said nothing, but Bibin seeing an opportunity to vent his anger, could not resist.

"When I came home earlier I found Manju taking something from under my bed. She was in my part of the room messing about with my things."

Talsi raised an inquisitive eyebrow as she looked at Manju.

"Is this true Manju? What were you doing?"

"Nothing," offered a floundering Manju. "I wasn't doing anything wrong, I was just…" But before she could finish Bibin seeking to further his advantage, intervened again.

"I told her. She has her own part of the room and I don't go in and interfere with her books, so she should leave my things alone. She had no right to be there."

"That's enough," ordered Talsi realising the necessity to quickly defuse the impending row, "I don't want to hear any more. When you have calmed down and are prepared to speak in reasonable tones I will talk to both of you and get to the bottom of this. Now let's finish our meal in a civilized manner"

The rest of the meal passed silently. Having cleared the plates and assisted her mother with washing up, Manju announced that she had homework to do and would go to her room, and afterwards have an early night. Bibin, still feeling ill-disposed towards his sister, left the house to practice catching a ball by bouncing it off the back wall of an adjacent building. Talsi, having decided that she could not face an argument that evening, felt some relief at the decisions made by her children and elected to wait until the following day to talk to each child individually, to understand the true source of Bibin's grievance and Manju's silence.

It was much later that evening that Bibin re-entered the scene of whatever crime it was he imagined Manju to have committed. Before climbing into bed, he reached beneath and pulled out the box containing his treasured cards. An evening of catching practice had caused him to wonder whether he might have given too little attention to some of the great Indian wicket keepers of the past. Perhaps Farokh Engineer deserved a place on his wall of honour, then there was Syed Kirmani much admired by his grandfather, or the great Gujarati Kiran More.

Opening the box Bibin began to search through the cards, looking for these fine wicket keepers amongst his collection. Here he first located Kiran More, whose record he compared with that of Dhoni who peered down at him from his place of honour on the wall. 110 catches in test matches, that is impressive, he muttered beneath his breath. Returning to his cards, thinking that his collection now appeared even larger than he had remembered, he continued searching until.., What was this? Taking a card from amongst the many others Bibin stared in disbelief. How could this be? Here in his hand he held the one card that he had sought for so many months.

Bibin needed to look at the card's detail for some time before he really believed that at last he held in his hand his missing hero, the great Sachin Tendulkar. Could this be true? But sure enough, there could be no doubt that here before him, was the clear image of India's greatest batsman. The joy which Bibin felt was immense as he realised that his collection was now complete. From now on there would be no more anxious visits to the corner shop, no more tearing open of packets only to be disappointed. Here before him, and ready for placing at the head of the wall, it really was Sachin Tendulkar.

As his excitement gradually subsided Bibin began to consider how this final missing card had come to enter his collection. Surely, he could not have overlook such a vital piece of the jigsaw that had been there all this time? Bibin turned over the events of the day in his mind. With this reflection came a realisation of the terrible injustice that he had committed against his sister. There could be no other explanation. When he had entered his room earlier and seen Manju kneeling beside his bed, he had quickly jumped to the wrong conclusion. Far from interfering with his property she had been engaged in an act of kindness. He realised now that it could only have been Manju who had added this card to the others in his box.

With mixed feelings of gratitude and remorse, Bibin leant across his bed and started to pull aside the curtain that divided the two halves of the room. This was the time to not only thank Manju, but also to offer a grovelling apology and seek her forgiveness for his earlier accusatory behaviour. Having realised that he had done her a great wrong he must not hesitate in putting matters right. Opening the curtain just enough so that he could see Manju lying on her bed he observed that she was sleeping soundly. He now felt both embarrassed and uncomfortable, knowing that tonight he would have to sleep aware of the terrible injustice that he had committed against his sister. He would have to wait until morning, before it would be possible to begin to make amends for his appalling behaviour. Turning once more to inspect the detail on his long sought card, Bibin lay back on his bed and reflected on how tomorrow he might ensure that both he and Manju had a better day.

The Tabla Teacher

Whenever he visited the house of his uncle and aunt in the Tondiarpet district of Chennai, Bibin liked to browse through the large collection of recordings of music, which his uncle had accumulated over many years. Uncle Nitin had eclectic tastes and within his library of discs were examples of both Indian and western music. In Bibin he recognised a kindred spirit who found pleasure in listening to the varied rhythms and voices that could be explored in this collection and he was pleased to encourage his nephew to seek out and play whatever he should choose.

Whilst during these infrequent visits to the city the adults appeared intent only on drinking chai and catching up with local gossip and his sister Manju was content to play with their cousins Sumathi and Jayashree, Bibin looked forward to being allowed to hunt through his uncle's collection to find those recordings, which he favoured and to possibly discover new and as yet unexplored discs. At home in Kalapurum access to records was limited and Bibin, who would have liked more opportunities to experience the variety of music, which he knew to be available beyond the boundaries of his small provincial town, relished these visits to his uncle's home. On these occasions after donning a pair of headphones and lying back against a deeply cushioned chair, he would become oblivious to all distractions and within a matter of minutes could lose himself in the music. Bibin liked to close his eyes and imagine himself present at a concert where the musicians on stage would be playing just for him.

Today's self-selected performance began with a compilation of jazz trumpet pieces played by the American musician Miles Davis. Uncle Nitin had many of this man's recordings and Bibin had often heard him describe the trumpeter as a genius. Bibin respected his uncle's views and persisted until the recording reached its conclusion, but at times the music sounded a little discordant to his untutored ears and he turned again to the collection to seek for more familiar sounds.

Sorting through a pile of plastic disc boxes Bibin looked for those names of known musicians that had given him pleasure during previous visits and he soon uncovered a recording that he felt sure would satisfy his need. The recording of a performance by the sitar maestro Nikhil Banerjee at a concert in Sweden had captured Bibin's imagination on earlier visits, and as he slipped the disc from its case and into the player he was confident that he could lie back and enjoy the warm tones created by this great musician. His anticipation was well rewarded and within minutes a familiar Hindustani classic was resonating through the headphones as the music gently coaxed him to follow its rhythm with a gentle tapping of his fingers against the arm of the chair. In this relaxed state Bibin was quickly immersed in the music, enjoying the virtuosity of Banerjee's playing with its rising and falling tones and repeated phrases. Lying back Bibin's whole body was possessed by the music, his head gently swaying, his fingers tapping and his steady breathing becoming one with the sounds washing over him. However, his attention suddenly shifted as the intensity of the tune was taken up by the tabla player who was now engaged in a fast exciting exchange with the principal musician as they seemed to vie for attention, locked in a musical conversation that at times bordered on the argumentative. First the sitar would dominate, asserting itself as the provider of the tune, but then, taking up the challenge the tabla assumed the upper hand until both musicians were galloping at a furious pace until eventually they appeared to harmonise in mutual respect.

Bibin opened his eyes and sitting up reached for the sleeve notes, which accompanied the disc. Reading down the list of musicians his attention was drawn to one name, that of Anindo Chatterjee the tabla player. It was not as if Bibin was not familiar with the tones and rhythms of the tabla; after all, this form of percussion was common in the performance of many Hindustani classics. But listening to this recording seemed to have awakened in Bibin a new consciousness; a sudden realisation of the power and majesty of the tabla player's art, which he had never previously appreciated. Here were rhythms that seemed to possess him, taking over every fibre of his being and causing him to become one with the music in a manner such as he had never experienced before. Sinking back into the chair Bibin once more closed his eyes and let the music flow around and through him, until finally the exchange between strings and percussion having reached its climax entered a period of reconciliation, calmed and concluded in a final gentle harmony.

Bibin was regarded by those who knew him best as a thoughtful and rational boy. Usually undemonstrative he was content to see outbursts of emotion as largely the domain of others and in particular that of his sister Manju. But that evening, as they waved goodbye to family and climbed aboard the bus that would return them in a couple of hours to their home in Kalapurum, Bibin found that he could not rid his mind of the excitement and the feelings that had owned him whilst listening to the music.

On the journey home Bibin was unusually quiet. So much so that his mother expressed concern that he might be feeling unwell. Perhaps, she speculated it is the motion of the bus over this rough potholed road that is causing the problem, though she could not recall a time when Bibin had ever suffered the nausea of travel sickness. Questioning her son Talsi enquired if he was indeed feeling unwell and when Bibin confirmed that he was fine, she decided that perhaps he was nothing more than a little tired at the end of what had been a long day. Even so, she decided to keep a watchful eye on him until they reached their home.

Bibin maintained his passive state until at last, approaching the outskirts of Kalapurum he broke his silence, and turning to his mother stated firmly, "I have made a decision. I am going to learn to play tabla."

Overhearing this statement, and before Talsi could reply to her son, Bibin's father leant forward from a seat across the aisle of the bus.

"Where has this come from?" he enquired. "When did you come by this idea?"

Bibin shifted in his seat and placing his hand in his trouser pocket pulled out a scrumpled piece of paper, which he carefully smoothed before pushing it towards his father.

"Here", he said. "I wrote this down this afternoon. It is the name of a great tabla player who I listened to on a disc at Uncle Nitin's house. His name is Anindo Chatterjee. I checked, he is on several discs in uncle's collection. The music he plays is wonderful and I am going to learn to play just like him."

Bibin's father looked at the paper in his hand and shook his head.

"Well," he began. "We will have to think about this. Learning to play an instrument requires great dedication and patience. We will have to see. Besides, where will you find the tabla? And more importantly, where will you find a teacher?"

"I don't know," replied Bibin. "But I will, I know I will."

***

A fortnight passed during which Bibin on several occasions in conversation with his parents, asserted his determination to learn to play tabla. Shortly after their return to Kalapurum his parents had assumed that this latest idea of Bibin's was nothing more than a passing fad. An idea provoked by listening to Nitin's record collection and one that would quickly fade. But gradually they came to appreciate that Bibin was being serious when he talked about the instrument and that he would not be satisfied until some effort had been made to provide him with at least an opportunity to recognise the challenges involved in becoming a musician.

It was a Friday evening when Bibin's father Anil arrived home after transporting the final fare of the day in his auto-rickshaw. Seeking out his son he informed him.

"One of my passengers today, a regular customer who I often pick up at the bus station, tells me that there is a man who lives in the last house in the lane that goes from behind the school towards Sethupathi Park. Apparently he teaches tabla and sometimes takes new students. I suppose that if you are serious about learning there would be no harm in you going to find this man. And if he is willing to take you as a student you could ask him how much are his fees. Of course, he may not be willing, and if he is too expensive, then I am afraid you will have to give up on your idea. And you must realise that we will need to know more about how much it costs to buy the tabla. If it is expensive then I am afraid that will have to be an end to your ambitions"

Bibin could hardly believe what he was hearing. He had thought that his father was opposed to the idea of him learning tabla and that he would put every object in his way. In all of their previous conversations he had appeared ill disposed to Bibin's new found enthusiasm. He had already recognised that there might be difficulties over the cost of lessons and had no idea of how he might obtain an instrument. But in Bibin's mind such obstacles were simply there to be overcome and could not detract from his determination. At times however, he felt that perhaps he was being unrealistic and had almost reconciled himself to not having the opportunity to learn, though despite his anxieties his enthusiasm had never dimmed. Turning to his father he said,

"I will go and find this man father as soon as I can. I will find out about lessons and what everything might cost. Only then will we be able to decide what to do. If this teacher is prepared to take me as a student and we can afford the costs, then I promise I will work hard to become a great player. You will see, one day I will make you proud"

Anil laughed; "Ok, you do that, but we are making no promises. There is no harm in you finding out more about this teacher, but don't take it for granted that we will be able to afford either the lessons or the instrument."

***

The following evening, at the end of the day's classes, Bibin made his way along the lane which snaked its way from the rear of the school towards Sethupathi Park. The small low roofed houses along this street were old and many were in a poor state of repair. These thought Bibin, do not look like the kind of houses where a great teacher might live. Bibin had walked here many times, but on previous occasions he had taken little notice of the individual buildings which bordered the road side. His father's passenger had indicated that the tabla teacher occupied the last house in the street, but Bibin wasn't sure and therefore seeing an elderly lady sitting in a doorway preparing vegetables, he approached and enquired of her whether she knew the man for whom he was looking. Hardly raising her head from her task to look at Bibin she raised an arm and waving in the direction of Sethupathi Park confirmed, "last house; there on the right."

Armed with this information and renewed confidence Bibin hurried on until he reached the threshold of the building that had been indicated by the woman. Here a door lacquered with peeling blue paint stood ajar and Bibin hesitated for a moment before summoning the conviction to knock. A few moments later a firm, deep voice came from within.

"Who's there? Who's that knocking?"

"Excuse me sir, my name is Bibin Sudev. I have come looking for the man who teaches tabla," replied Bibin somewhat apprehensively.

"Is that so?" came the reply. "Well, in that case you had better come in."

Bibin pushed gingerly at the half open door and entered the low ceilinged room, his eyes struggling to adjust to the gloom when leaving the bright afternoon sunlight behind. The room was in almost total darkness, with just a shaft of light falling to the floor from a chink in the wall to his right. Squinting in the blackness of the room, Bibin could discern only the vague shape of a person sitting largely obscured in the murkiness that dominated the house, near the far wall, opposite where he stood. This he surmised must be the tabla teacher. Between this shadowy figure and himself on the floor Bibin could just make out a number of percussion instruments, a couple of which he recognised as similar to those played by performers in the pictures, accompanying some of his uncle Nitin's recordings. Here immediately before him lay a long laced mridangam and beside this a decorated wooden dholak, but his attention was particularly drawn to a fine banjara tabla carefully balanced upon red leather cushions, which occupied the ground immediately in front of the man who he assumed to be the teacher.

"So young man, you think you might learn to play tabla, is that right?" asked the man from his gloomy position ten feet away from Bibin.

"Yes sir," answered Bibin. "I was told that you might be taking students who were keen to learn, and I was hoping that you could teach me."

"Is that so?" continued the teacher. "Well, I don't just take anybody as a student. Learning tabla is a hard pathway and I will have to be sure that you are prepared to follow such a difficult route. You will need to show me what you can do. Come now, sit where you are and listen."

Bibin did as he was told and seated himself cross legged on the ground. As he did so the teacher began to clap a simple rhythm before commanding him to produce the same pattern.

This Bibin did with ease and was therefore not surprised when the rhythm was changed to one of a different emphasis and beat. Adjusting to this change Bibin again imitated the sounds produced by the teacher who offered no comment before launching into a rather more complex set of rhythms requiring Bibin to once more accommodate the change.

This procedure continued for several more minutes with the teacher leading the way and Bibin doing his best to follow until eventually he recognised that he was beginning to struggle to give an exact rendition of the rhythm created by the master.

"Stop," commanded the teacher suddenly before falling into a silence, which whilst lasting no more than a couple of minutes seemed to Bibin to continue for an eternity. Finally the quiet was broken as the master stated, "you have good rhythm. You may have potential, though many who begin well fall from the path when the demands increase. But you seem to be a serious boy and I have therefore decided that I will take you as a student for a two month trial. If at the end of that period you have satisfied me that you have the aptitude and the dedication required to play tabla, I may commit myself to become your guru. But you must recognise that many begin this pathway and few continue. I will expect you to show commitment and to abide by the discipline that I will demand. If I detect any deviation from the path which I set you upon, then I will end our association. Is that clear?"

Bibin listened to these words carefully, recognising that he had passed a test that had the potential to give him access to a new and exciting world. He also appreciated the gravity and the firmness with which this message had been conveyed. Hardly knowing how to respond he blurted out a series of almost incomprehensible statements.

"Thank you sir, yes thank you. Of course sir, I will work hard sir, I promise. Thank you, thank you."

Raising his hand the teacher indicated that Bibin should cease his effusive noise.

"Two months I say. After this we will review your progress. I make no promises beyond two months, do you understand that?"

"I understand sir. Yes sir, two months. I will work hard I promise," stuttered Bibin, but then remembering his father's words he knew he must ask the questions which might yet thwart his musical ambitions.

"I'm sorry sir, but my father tells me I must ask. I hope you do not mind me asking sir. How much will I have to pay? Where will I obtain the tabla?"

Once more raising a hand the teacher replied. "For two months you will work hard and there will be no fee. When the time is right and if you prove yourself worthy, I will provide you with the tabla, though that may not be for several weeks, if at all. After this, but only if you reach my standards, if I take you as my student we will come to an arrangement. You may see from the simple way in which I live I am a teacher and not a businessman. If you have the talent, then we will manage."

Bibin could hardly believe his luck. Not only had he found a teacher, but the man was prepared to give him his initial lessons for no charge. This was far more than he had dared to hope for. Thanking the teacher once again he began to raise himself from the floor in order to take his leave.

"We will begin on Sunday evening. Be here sharp at six o'clock and do not be late. I will not tolerate indiscipline and that means being here on time." The teacher's voice was firm and Bibin realised that this was a man who was serious about his work. "Now you may go and remember, Sunday at six and don't be late."

Bibin having risen from the floor promised that he would be on time and turned to take his leave. He got as far as the door when the teacher's voice rang out again ordering him once more to stop.

"Please wait," commanded the teacher, though in a tone much softer than that heard up until now. "There is something you can do for me. Please go outside and you will see a small box against the wall of the house just beside the door. Open the box and see if there is a letter contained within this for me."

Bibin immediately exited the door and finding the box opened it to reveal that there was indeed a single letter in a brown Manilla envelope lying at the bottom. Returning to the house with the letter Bibin began to cross the room to the teacher, but before he had made much progress the man issued a further command.

"Please stay there. Well, I detect from your approach that there is a letter. Would you then please do me the service of opening it and reading its contents to me?"

Bibin hesitated; was this some further test he wondered? Why should the teacher expect him to read his correspondence? If he stumbled in his reading would the teacher now change his mind and refuse to give him lessons? Confused but not wishing to challenge his new found teacher and possibly jeopardise this relationship from the outset, Bibin began carefully to undo the envelope and to reveal its contents.

"Please read," instructed the teacher, this time in a much more gentle voice.

Bibin turned the letter to catch the little light that illuminated the room. He scanned the letter before him before taking a deep breath and reading its contents aloud. The letter notified the listener of a forthcoming festival to be held in Bangalore, an event at which three of the teacher's former students would be performing. It invited him to attend and informed him that he would be welcome as a guest of the festival organisers who would provide suitable accommodation and transport. Having finished his reading Bibin returned the letter to the envelope.

"Thank you," said the teacher. "I am most grateful for your assistance."

"Did I pass the test?" asked Bibin.

"The test?" enquired the teacher. "Do you mean the rhythm exercise?"

"No sir," replied Bibin. "I just wondered, was the letter reading some kind of test?"

The teacher laughed. "Oh no, that was not a test. I simply needed you to read the letter for me because I am unable to do this for myself. You see I am completely blind. I cannot see anything more than vague shadows and I am certainly not able to read a letter."

Bibin was taken aback, somewhat embarrassed and unsure what he should say, but as the teacher left a silence in the room he felt that he should at least say something.

"I'm sorry sir," began Bibin. "I didn't realise. I mean I hadn't noticed."

"Why should you have?" the teacher responded, sensing Bibin's discomfort and trying to put him at ease. "I gave you no reason to think that I was blind and it had no bearing upon our conversation. But I detect now that you are rather surprised to discover my blindness. Am I right?"

"Well, yes sir. I suppose you are really," stuttered Bibin, "but I didn't mean to be rude."

"And do you think perhaps my blindness really matters?" asked the teacher.

"Well sir, I don't know. I mean I suppose I just didn't expect. You see sir; I have never before met a teacher who is blind. I guess I was just wondering, how difficult must it be for someone who is blind to be a teacher."

"Yes, I see," said the blind teacher. "I don't suppose there are too many of us around. But you shouldn't let my blindness be of concern. You see, I have always personally found that vision is far more important than sight. Wouldn't you agree?"

Bibin was silent.

"Ah," said the teacher. "I can see that those words have left you a little confused. Well young man, go home and think about what I have just said, and perhaps when you return for your first lesson on Sunday you too will be able to see more clearly than you can at present."

Bibin left his new teacher's home thinking that this next chapter in his life was destined to be a great adventure; possibly even in ways that he might never previously have imagined.

Incident on Platform 2A

It wasn't often that the Sudev family travelled together by train. Seated on the platform at Chennai Central station amidst the heap of baggage that constituted their luggage, Talsi, Anil, Bibin and Manju eagerly anticipated the long journey ahead, and to meeting family and friends when they eventually reached Basavanagudi in Bangalore. For the past six months they had been looking forward to this day, and more particularly to attending the marriage of Tulsi's niece Sonali to Anuvesh who had a tailoring business in the great Karnataka city. They had arrived early at the station in the Periyamet district in Chennai, and Bibin was already displaying the symptoms of restlessness, which come with the boredom of awaiting a much-anticipated event.

Manju's approach to any long wait, whether it be at a bus stop in Kalapurum, in a queue for a cinema ticket, or seated on a railway platform, was simple and consistent. Immediately on arrival she had taken from her bag one of several books that would accompany her for the next week and had immersed herself in its pages. Bibin, less inclined to adopt such a studious approach, found it difficult to settle and with his mother's anxious warning that he should not wander out of sight ringing in his ears, he explored the immediate environs of the platform seeking some diversion without knowing what this might be or from whence it might emerge.

No matter what the time of day Chennai Central station is busy. The bustle of passengers scouring the platforms seeking their correct position for departure, the vendors plying their trade with loud cries of "chai, chai, chai" or "coffee, coffee" and the red shirted porters bearing with apparent ease their heavy burdens atop their heads, made for a colourful spectacle, though none could hold Bibin's interest for more than a few minutes.

Reluctantly returning to the family group, having discovered nothing of especial interest, Bibin slumped beside his sister and commenced occupying himself by irritating Manju through an interruption of her reading; an act that he correctly calculated would elicit a negative response.

"Isn't it boring, just sitting here waiting?" he commenced. "Nothing to do; how much longer will we have to wait?"

"I have another book in my bag if you want to borrow it," replied Manju, forcing herself to hide her irritation and not looking up from her current page.

"Another book! How many books do you need for a journey Manju? You can't read more than one at a time. Anyway, it's too noisy and busy to read."

Manju half turned so that she had her annoying elder brother at her back, giving a clear signal that she wanted to be left in peace. However, she immediately realised that this was a mistake as poking his sister in the ribs Bibin recommenced his verbal assault.

"Hey, don't turn your back on me when I'm speaking to you. That's not nice."

Manju had to conceded that this had perhaps been a bad-mannered move. With a sigh she accepted that her reading was albeit temporarily, to be suspended and she therefore noted her page with a bookmark and returned the book to her bag.

"I'm sorry," Manju apologised, then pointing to the platform clock in an attempt to calm her restless brother, "It won't be long now. Thirty minutes and they should start allowing us to board the train."

Bibin heaved a loud sigh but acknowledging his sister's attempt to make a truce, tried to engage her in more friendly conversation.

"So many people; this station is always too busy, don't you think?" he asked.

"India has too many people everywhere," observed his sister. "There is so little space left anywhere in the city, and nowhere that is quiet."

A sensible peace having been brokered, the siblings continued their semi-philosophical discussion about the situation in their country, when they noticed a uniformed officer wearing the insignia and three chevrons indicating his rank as a head constable in the Indian Police Service, swaggering purposefully along the platform in their direction. As he drew nearer the two younger members of the Sudev family felt a sense of relief, not through any sense of guilt, but rather as a result of an innate respect for figures of authority, as they noticed that he was quickening his step to attend to a situation further along the platform and had no interest in them. Turning to watch his progress their attention was swiftly drawn to two other characters who were destined to become central actors in a drama that was about to enfold. The first, a young woman, dressed in western style with tightly fitting blue jeans, red trainers and a red t-shirt was being accosted by the second, an elderly and dishevelled, disabled man who leant awkwardly on a single wooden crutch as he held out his hand towards the woman in an act of supplication.

Neither of these two players in the drama appeared to have observed the policeman hastening along the platform, and certainly not to have anticipated the force with which he brought down his lathi across the back of the disabled beggar. The power of the blow, taking the elderly man by surprise caused him to lurch forward and fall at the feet of the startled young woman who stepped backwards and uttered a loud yelp. A further blow from the officer's lathi as the beggar attempted to regain his feet, sent him scurrying along the platform accompanied by a series of vicious oaths fired in his direction by his assailant.

Bibin and Manju looked to each other in horror at what they had just witnessed. Beggars they knew could be a nuisance and even at times a little intimidating, but neither of them believed that the actions of the officer were justified as a means of addressing this situation. Manju winced and muttered, quietly enough to ensure that whilst Bibin could hear, the offensive officer could not.

"What a bully. Beating him like that wasn't necessary. He wasn't threatening the woman and she looks as if she could easily have handled the situation herself."

Bibin agreed and observing the policeman carefully added his own interpretation of the situation.

"Now look at him. See the way he is smiling at the woman. Can you see how he is showing off to her, making out that he rescued her from some evil that was about to take place. He only got involved because he wanted to impress her. Look at him trying to chat her up"

Brother and sister continued to watch the officer whose behaviour confirmed Bibin's assertion that he was making extraordinary efforts to ingratiate himself with the attractive young woman. As they watched they noted how he adopted an unctuous smile as he chatted in an apparently casual manner with the woman who seemed to be uncomfortable and unsure of how she should react. He behaves, thought Manju, like some brave knight from a story book who has just rescued a damsel in distress from a fire breathing dragon, rather than the bully that he really is. His behaviour she decided, was beyond contempt as he used the authority invested in him through his uniform to play a role, rather than to do his duty.

Whilst Bibin and Manju continued to adopt their condemnatory position they noticed that the young woman had quite suddenly turned away from the policeman, her attention distracted by something or someone further along the platform. Following the direction of her gaze, they saw a tall young man calling a name and dodging between the crowd as he hurried towards her. On hearing the call and locating the oncoming man, the woman waved excitedly in his direction and ran to greet him. Within a few seconds they were clutching each other in an affectionate embrace, the newcomer lifting her off her feet and swinging her around as he held her close to him.

Bibin smiled as he observed that the police officer had begun to depart the scene, shaking his head and muttering inaudibly. He nudged Manju and laughed, as he suggested that perhaps some kind of justice had been served. His sister agreed as they watched the young couple now hand in hand, smiling and engaged in animated conversation.

Bibin turned to observe the departing policeman who was walking towards a bench located at the back of the platform. Here were seated two elderly ladies well laden with canvas bags. As the policeman reached them he whipped the edge of the bench hard with his lathi making a clatter that resonated across the platform. Barking a command, the detail of which was lost in the general hubbub of the station, but the meaning of which was clear enough to both Bibin and his sister, they watched as the elderly ladies meekly vacated the seat in order that the officer could claim it as his own.

"I said that man was a bully," stated Manju. "Now we have it confirmed. What a horrible man."

As she said this the officer settled back on the bench, propping his lathi beside him and casting his eyes around, possibly thought Manju, looking for further opportunities for confrontation. But as she watched the bullying policeman he leaned back, pulled his cap forward over his eyes and appeared to be intent on getting some sleep. Most policemen she knew, did not behave in this appalling manner, but this man was one to avoid. Best let sleeping dogs lie.

Bibin looked up to the platform clock. Ten minutes until boarding.

"Yes, he certainly is a bully," he confirmed. "But I think we could teach him a lesson, don't you?"

Manju had heard this tone from Bibin before, and whilst she agreed that it would be good to bring the officer down a little, she was apprehensive that her brother's impetuosity could lead to trouble. Bibin sensed her anxiety but having hatched a scheme he was not to be easily thwarted.

"Listen Manju, all I need you to do is keep Appa and Amma busy for two minutes. Just make sure that they are not looking in the direction of the policeman. That's all I am asking. I promise you will not get into trouble."

Manju was about to make a good case for why she thought Bibin should forget the incident, when he rose to his feet and with a nod of the head moved off in the direction of the snoozing officer. Realising that whatever plan Bibin had in mind would be jeopardised unless she played her part, she took her book out of her bag, opened it and declared to her parents that she wished to read something to them.

"Listen," she demanded, "I read this passage earlier. It describes how beautiful the Kashmir Valley is in the spring Let me read it to you." And keeping an eye on the actions of her brother she commenced to read and to hold her parents' attention.

Bibin approached the bench upon which his intended victim slouched with stealth and more than a little apprehension. When eventually he stood before the officer and had assured himself that he was indeed oblivious to his presence, he looked around to confirm that his next move could be made with minimal risk. Only when confident that his scheme would succeed did Bibin act. Without hesitation he grasped the lathi from its position leaning against the bench and swiftly dashed a few yards along the platform, to where a large wheeled bin full of rubbish awaiting collection was standing. Quickly lifting the lid, he dropped the lathi in to the receptacle and buried it beneath an empty sack and other detritus before once more closing it.

Manju who had been watching Bibin's mission whilst also trying to hold her parents' attention, could feel her heart racing and was relieved when Bibin re-joined the family group without having disturbed his sleeping victim. He nodded to her as he arrived, and she smiled back at him, indicating her approval and confirming her complicity in the deed.

It was only ten minutes later as the Sudev family climbed aboard the train that Manju and Bibin finally felt that they were safe from being discovered as culprits in a crime against the officer. A felony of which they were certainly guilty but for the committing of which, neither of them had any regrets. Bibin thought Manju, has acted to punish a bully and my participation in this event was therefore fully justified.

Staring through the carriage window as the train's first lurch indicated that they would soon be departing from Chennai, they watched as the policeman stirred himself, having been disturbed by the noise from the engine. Sitting upright and repositioning his cap firmly in place he took an overview of the platform, its inhabitants and all that was happening around him. Scanning the scene before him he was taken aback, when there less than ten metres in front of him, he regarded again that same beggar who he had dealt with earlier. Enraged by the audacity demonstrated by this man who had returned to beg despite his earlier punishment, the policeman reached down for his lathi, intent on teaching this reprobate a much more severe lesson.

As the train pulled away from the platform Anil turned to his children curious to know what had made them suddenly laugh so uproariously. Manju and Bibin didn't dare explain how they had watched the policeman desperately searching first under the bench and then frantically behind and beneath various other obstacles located along the platform. As he did so, two members of the railway cleaning staff commenced to push the wheeled rubbish bin towards the station exit. Neither child could openly express the joy they had felt in seeing the young woman and her boyfriend returning along the platform, where on once again encountering the beggar they stopped and handed him what they assumed to be a few coins.

Turning to her parents and knowing that her father demanded an answer to his question about their laughter, Manju reported,

"Bibin and I are just excited about going to the wedding in Bangalore. We have been waiting on the platform for so long, we were laughing with relief that we are now on the train." This, she believed was not a lie, though neither was it exactly the whole truth. She liked to think that had he known the full story, her father would have agreed that justice had been served upon a bully, but she knew better than to test her theory at this precise moment.

The Letter

Mrs Gupta missed her son Pavan with the kind of ache that can only be known by a loving mother. At first, when he left home following terrible scenes of rage and violent confrontation with his father, she feared that she would never hear from Pavan again. Everything had happened so suddenly that evening, leaving Anoushka Gupta distressed and confused. There had been little indication of the precursor to those traumatic scenes, which had blighted her life since the day of his departure. It was not only that the events of that fateful evening had been so unexpected that had hurt so much, but the fact that ever since that time she had been expected to live without understanding what had led to her son's sudden banishment.

It had always seemed to her that Pavan had been contented with his life in Kalapurum, with so many friends and interests. Nothing could have prepared her for the terrible shouting that she had overheard from the street as she had arrived home from the church service she had been attending that night. She had entered the house full of apprehension, and this was heightened when suddenly aware of her presence, her husband and son had paused their angry altercation, Pavan turning towards his mother and proffering a muttered apology before dashing from the room, leaving Anoushka to confront her husband, who could barely control his shaking.

Anoushka wanted an explanation, but before she could demand this of her husband he raised his hand and shook his head, indicating firmly that he did not wish to engage with her in any form of discussion. Turning his back he too left the room, the slamming of the door indicating that in his mind he was bringing closure to the evening's events. Within an hour Pavan was gone. Anoushka heard nothing of his departure as he crept from the house and it was the following day before she realised that he had packed a bag with just a few personal items and left home.

By the time of her realisation, Anoushka's husband had departed for his work and it was not until later that day that she was able to seek from him an explanation of the previous evening's events. Until that day they had always been able to discuss every aspect of their lives together. Theirs had been a harmonious household in which, when troubles arose they were shared and a solution sought by falling back on the strength of their family resources. She was therefore stunned when her husband stood before her and stated bluntly that he never again wished to have Pavan's name mentioned in his hearing. That as far as he was concerned, they no longer had a son and she would do well to forget that he had ever been a part of the household. Anoushka was stunned and at first persisted with efforts to discover what had passed between her husband and her son, but these were greeted with anger such as she had never experienced in thirty years of marriage and she realised the futility of continuing along this path.

The next few weeks, with no news of Pavan, Anoushka lived her life in a daze. Unable to comprehend the causes of this terrible schism, she found herself struggling to concentrate on even the most trivial of tasks. Worn down by her grief it seemed impossible to discuss the situation even with her closest friends and family for fear that she might invoke the wrath of her husband. How she wondered, could one terrible evening so alter the course of their lives? Was she in any way to blame for the furious argument that she had so nearly witnessed between the two most precious men in her life? For many weeks, these and similar questions took possession of her thoughts and she lived her life in despair and anguish.

At last there came news that brought her some relief. It was three months since Pavan's departure, a period during which she had begun to wonder if she would ever see or hear from him again. But then when she was about to lose all hope, as she was leaving her work at the fish market one evening, Sachin a young man who had been Pavan's closest friend all through his school years approached her in the street.

"Mrs Gupta," he began. "I'm glad I have found you. I have had word from Pavan. He asked me to see you and to let you know that he is well. He is in England where he has a job. He says that he will send word to you very soon and that you are not to worry." Anoushka wanted to hug Sachin so grateful was she for this news, however unexpected and brief. But welcome as his words were, they had stunned her and before she could express her gratitude Sachin had turned and was gone, heading across the busy road.

Hurrying home after this brief meeting with Sachin, Anoushka found herself in tears. She was not sure whether these were tears of relief or of sorrow and in truth they may well have been both. Pavan in England; so far away. What could have driven him to go so far? But thank God at least she had heard from him at last. Pavan is safe and he is well and that alone would bring her some relief. Should she tell her husband what she had heard? Anoushka was confused by the brief message conveyed by Pavan's friend, but on this last point it took little time to decide that she would say nothing. She would keep this glad news to herself. On the few occasions that Pavan's name had been mentioned in his hearing in recent months her husband had become angry and she did not wish to cause either of them more pain.

Anoushka blessed the day that Sachin had brought her news. The details were sparse, but at least she knew that Pavan was safe, and just as Sachin had predicted, within a few days a letter from her son arrived in Kalapurum to bring her further comfort. After this initial renewal of contact, letters came often if not regularly, to reassure her that he was indeed well and adjusting to a new life away from home. Before long Anoushka recognised and had begun to accept that Pavan was settled and likely to stay in England. He had a good job with an advertising agency in Birmingham and as she waited impatiently for the letters, which would arrive most months bringing her news of his life so far away, she was grateful that her son appeared happy and safe, even if he was at so great a distance from home. Gradually her anxiety, though never fully eliminated, eased and as time passed she felt reassured that Pavan was forging a new life for himself in England.

The letters were always delivered to the home of Mrs Gupta's friend Talsi who would summon her in order to read to her the latest word from her estranged son. Anoushka who never having had the benefit of attending school was unable to read the letters for herself, was certain that should they fall into the hands of her husband they would be destroyed before she received the words that helped to ease her pain and she was grateful to Talsi for playing the role of an intermediary. Even today, almost two years after Pavan had left their home, Anoushka's husband refused to tell her the cause of the rift between father and son and she knew that to raise the issue would provoke his anger. Talsi Sudev, though several years her junior was a good friend. Pavan knew that his mother and Mrs Sudev were close and had rightly surmised that she would act wisely in order to support her by conveying his news in confidence and with reassurance. Most importantly, Talsi was someone upon whom Anoushka knew she could depend for discretion and understanding, and she was grateful that she was willing to allow Pavan's letters to be sent to her home. At times she felt guilty for drawing Talsi into this secretive situation, but her friend reassured her that she would always act with discretion and Anoushka knew that she could trust her. After each reading of a letter Anoushka would entrust the letters to Talsi's care, knowing that she would keep them safe and that there was no danger of her husband ever finding them.

It was as she was leaving the fish market at the end of a morning's work one Friday that Mrs Gupta heard her name being called; "Anoushka, Anoushka." She turned and looked around before locating Talsi who was waving from across the traffic choked road and then waited until a break in the hustling flow enabled her to hurry across to her friend, who was waiting near the entrance to Sethupathi Park.

"I thought I had missed you," declared Talsi. "I looked around the market but you must have just left your place. I'm glad to have found you because I knew you would want to know as soon as possible that another letter has come from Pavan. It arrived yesterday and I was sure you would be waiting."

Anoushka Gupta took Talsi urgently by the hand, "thank you, thank you so much, do you have the letter here?"

"Yes, it's right here," said Talsi, indicating the bag that was suspended from her shoulder. "Come into the park, we can find a bench and I will read it to you."

Mrs Gupta looked all around her. She knew that this was a moment of intrigue and that no matter how many times such events were repeated, she would still feel that she was involved in an act of treachery towards her husband. Talsi understood this situation well, and as on many previous occasions tried to offer reassurance that the act in which she too was about to play a major role would never be disclosed. Together they entered the park, Anoushka hurriedly leading the way to where she knew a bench could be found, which being beneath the overhanging branches of a broad-leaved catalpa tree would shield them from curious observers. Even then, on arrival at the seat it was necessary to check in all directions to ensure that this subversive tryst was unlikely to attract unwanted attention.

Once established on the bench Talsi rummaged through the contents of her bag until at last the long awaited letter was retrieved. Snatching it from Talsi's grasp Mrs Gupta held it in trembling hands, staring at the unopened envelope as if suspicious that what she saw might be something other than the anticipated missal from her son. Though unable to read she had become familiar with the formation of letters that confirmed beyond doubt that this was indeed word from Pavan.

Her contemplation of the envelope didn't last long before with words that betrayed her impatience she whispered surreptitiously, "Please, read it to me, I want to know all of Pavan's news." So saying, Anoushka thrust the letter eagerly towards Talsi.

"But first you must open the letter," insisted Talsi pushing the object back in Anoushka's direction. "It is addressed to you and it would not feel right if I should open the envelope. Please, you know how I feel about this; you must do this and take the letter from inside. Then I will be very happy to read for you." Talsi offered a reassuring smile enabling Anoushka to understand the sincerity of her words.

Anoushka knew that this was their familiar ritual and therefore reclaimed the letter from her friend and placing it on her lap smoothed and stared at it for a moment as if gaining the courage to release the contents from within the envelope. At this precise moment this was her most treasured possession and she needed to be sure to handle it with the care and respect that it deserved. When at last she recovered from her reverie, with trembling hands she tore the envelope open and withdrew two blue pages of paper and handing these to Talsi urged her.

"Please, I can wait no longer. I need to know what Pavan has to say."

Talsi held the pages before her and began to read in a low conspiratorial voice, knowing of the need to maintain secrecy. As is the nature of letters to family, the opening phrases were those of endearment and reassurance. Talsi's reading assured Anoushka that Pavan was well, although he still found the climate in Birmingham cold. He was adjusting well to life in England and felt settled in the city. His job too was going well, in fact he had received a small promotion and his employers were pleased with his work. He had developed an interest in football and sometimes went to see a game at the Aston Villa club, though he looked forward to the English summer when he could resume his passion for cricket and maybe even attend a test match at the ground in Edgbaston, which wasn't far from where he was living.

Such domestic news was familiar to Talsi who recognised a comforting pattern to Pavan's letters, in which he wrote positively of his life in England in order to offer the relief which he knew his mother would crave. Talsi looked up from the letter to see that despite the tears in her eyes Anoushka was smiling; an indication she thought that she was relieved by the words that she was hearing. She resumed her reading of the letter which continued in similar vein throughout the first page, interrupted only when Anoushka interjected.

"He is doing so well. Do you see he has been given a promotion? I knew he would do well, he has always been a clever and a hard working boy."

Talsi smiled and nodded reassuringly before turning to the second page of the letter, the first few lines of which appeared to contain yet more good news. Pavan reported that he was very happy having found a partner who was now sharing the apartment that he rented in Birmingham. He was sure that his mother would be very pleased for him because he was thrilled to have established what he knew would be a loving and lifelong relationship.

Talsi paused and looked up from the letter. Mrs Gupta turned her face towards her and at first, whilst appearing to want to say something, remained silent as if searching for appropriate words. A look of confusion passed across Anoushka's face and Talsi turned back to the letter knowing that a barrage of questions was likely to follow. Eventually after what seemed to Talsi like a longer pause than had in fact been the case, Anoushka at last stuttered.

"A partner? A loving relationship? What does this mean, what more does he say?" Anoushka looked anxiously to Talsi to provide clarification, urging her to continue.

During this brief hiatus as Anoushka had been juggling her thoughts Talsi had read ahead, and now she too found herself struggling for the right words, uncertain how she should proceed with the task that she had previously been so pleased to undertake on Mrs Gupta's behalf. Suddenly she found that the favour, which she had so willingly begun, was turning into something less palatable. But having taken on this role she knew that she must find a way forward.

"The things that he has to say," she finally stated, "are very personal. The words were written just for you and I'm not sure how he would feel about me reading his letter." Talsi knew as soon as she had uttered these words that it was too late to withdraw from her responsibilities. She was looking for an escape which she realised would not be available to her. She had agreed the role of interpreter and now she would have to see her mission to a conclusion. Anoushka had always been happy to share the confidences that existed between a mother and son and would not understand if now she shirked from this task.

"Please," urged Mrs Gupta, "I need to know. You always read his letters to me and I am so grateful. There are no secrets between you and me. Without your help I would never be able to know Pavan's news. Please read to me exactly what Pavan says in his letter. Please use his words." Lowering her voice she looked once more around her checking that no one could overhear, "whatever he says I need to know. I need to know about this loving partner, who is she? What does he say about her?"

Talsi looked anxious and hoped that her discomfort didn't betray her emotions. Having weighed the situation in her mind she had concluded that there was little option and she resolved that the best course of action would be to read the words exactly as written by Pavan. To do otherwise might lead to greater misunderstanding and could possibly become a cause of considerable distress. Despite her apprehension she could see no alternative other than possibly to tell her friend a lie. But if she were to follow this deceitful path it would be only a matter of time before her dishonesty would be discovered. Taking a deep breath she continued with her reading.

"My partner," she read, "is named David. He is two years older than me and works as a laboratory technician at the university."

Talsi's reading was interrupted by a stifled gasp from her friend, who reeling back on the bench hid her face behind her hands, an act that did little to conceal the obvious anguish with which Anoushka was suddenly gripped. Talsi leant towards her, placing a gentle hand on her shoulder and asking, "should I continue? Would you rather I stopped?" Anoushka said nothing at first, but after a few seconds shook her head, urging her friend to continue and with this Talsi decided that it would be best to precis the text in order to quickly reach the letter's conclusion.

"Pavan says that in England now, the law makes it possible for he and David to marry, and that they intend doing so in the spring. He knows that this will come as a shock to you, but he wants you to be happy for him. He says that he knows that you love him and will want him to be happy. He realises that it may take some time for you to understand, but he knows that you will want what is best for him. He wants you to know that with David he has found great happiness and love. He also says that he realises that if he hears this news his father will be angry, but that he will possibly be less surprised than you. Pavan says he loves you very much and hopes that one day he will be able to fly you to England and that you will see him again and meet David."

Talsi was aware of her hands shaking as she folded the letter carefully and returned it to the envelope. Looking at Anoushka she found herself groping for appropriate words as she watched her friend sobbing and wiping tears from her eyes. Eventually however, it was Mrs Gupta who broke the silence.

"Thank you" she began, clearly determined to create an illusion of inner calm. "You are a good friend Talsi and I would not have wished for anyone else to tell me Pavan's good news. He is my son and he is doing well and that is what matters. I cannot understand how things are so far away in England, I know that things are different there, but he says that he is happy and he is doing well. What more should a mother wish for? He has received a promotion at his work and that is good. You read what he said, he is happy and doing well. When his next letter comes you will be able to tell me more of his news. Thank you Talsi, you are such a good friend. Now I must go home. I must go and prepare a meal for my husband. He, of course must never know Pavan's good news. He might be proud that Pavan has gained promotion in his job, but he must never know. He must never find out that I receive these letters from Pavan in England and he must never know either about… well you know that he must never know anything at all".

"Please Talsi, what you must do now is take the letter and make sure it is burned so that no one else can ever read it. The good news which Pavan has sent is just for his mother, though I am of course pleased to share this news with you. You are a good friend and I thank you for reading Pavan's news. I hope that soon he will write again and that I will have more good news from England. Now I must go, so thank you, thank you so much"

Talsi watched silently, lost for words as Mrs Gupta rose from the bench and after placing a grateful hand upon her friends shoulder, indicated that there was nothing more to be said. With her head held high Anoushka strode purposefully towards the exit of Sethupathi Park and made her way home contemplating the good news that she had received from Pavan in England.

A School for All

1.

Friday mornings at Dr. Ambedkar School in Kalapurum always began with students and teachers gathered in the courtyard at the front of the main building. Here the head teacher, Mr Desai would lead those assembled in the singing of the school song, a ritual that was always followed by a reporting of school news, often singling out individual students for praise for some academic or sporting achievement or for having made a contribution to a community event.

Bibin and Maju always looked forward to this gathering, though both regarded the event positively for different reasons. For Manju, the assembly provided an opportunity to hear about what her fellow students had been doing and to share in the celebration of good works and outstanding achievements. She had on occasions been personally singled out for her own school performance, or for some activity in which she had excelled outside of school. For Bibin, this being a Friday morning occurrence, it came with the joyful thought that tomorrow being Saturday, he would be free from what he saw as the restrictive environment of the school.

The pattern for the weekly school assembly was well established and rarely veered from its expected course. In most respects today's meeting was no different. However a rumour had been circulating for the past week that Mr Desai was going to make an important announcement. Nobody really knew where this rumour had begun, though it had prompted much speculation amongst the students. Some had hopefully suggested that there might be an announcement about an additional school holiday, though no one could say quite why this should be the case. The more pessimistic predicted an additional examination to be added to the annual end of year assessment format. Though again, they discussed this possibility on the basis of scant evidence.

It may have been that the anticipation of this rumoured announcement gave cause for every student to be particularly focused during this morning's gathering, and indeed when Mr Desai stepped forward and stated that he had something important to say, he immediately commanded the attention of all present. Scanning the gathered audience before him, the principal cleared his throat and with his usual deep authoritative tone began his speech.

"As some of you here may well be aware," he began, "At the start of next academic year, it will be twenty years since Dr Ambedkar School opened. This is indeed a momentous occasion and one for which the people of Kalapurum have much reason to celebrate. As I look over those of you standing before me today, I am reminded that for many of your parents, school attendance previously required them to make long journeys into Chennai. Sadly, for many this was not always possible and this meant that many were unable to obtain the education that they needed and deserved. The opening of this school twenty years ago was a momentous event in the life of this small community. It ensured that for the first time, all children who live within the boundaries of Kalapurum were able to attend their own local school."

At this moment, led by a number of enthusiastic teachers, the gathered assembly engaged in a loud round of applause. Having decided that this sign of appreciation had achieved the desired appreciative effect, Mr Desai raised his hand to indicate the need for silence as he had more to say.

"Such an important anniversary must not be allowed to pass without recognition," he continued. "Having discussed this matter with the teachers, we have decided that we will hold an open day at the beginning of the new school year, so that all residents of Kalapurum have an opportunity to come and see the excellent work that you do and to celebrate your achievements. However, we would also like to receive suggestions from you, the students of this school, about other events that we might hold during next year, which should be an extended period of celebration. I would therefore be grateful if you would all give some consideration to how we might mark this anniversary and bring your ideas to me in order that we can make plans. The importance of this next year in the history of Kalapurum should be recognised across the community. It was only with the coming of this school that we were able at last to guarantee an education for every child who lives here. So please give this occasion some thought and come to me with your ideas."

The announcement over, Mr Desai dismissed the assembly and the students made their way to their classes, many already pondering the kind of events that might be planned for this important celebratory year.

2.

Unsurprisingly Mr Desai's announcement provoked a great deal of discussion among the students over the coming days. So it was that a few days later, sitting on the school field a group of friends began to share some of their thoughts about the kinds of events that might be appropriate for celebrating this auspicious anniversary. Nobody was surprised when Bibin suggested that a cricket match might be a fitting way to mark the occasion. After all, many of the school's current and past students were keen players. Perhaps a match between current and past students would be a good idea. This proposal met with general approval, as did others suggesting concerts, theatre performances and a sports day to include the participation of parents. Manju proposed that a commemorative book telling the history of the school and the achievements of past students would provide a more permanent way of celebrating the year. This could contain a series of recollections, photographs and pen portraits of distinguished alumni and might involve current students interviewing those from a previous generation.

The general enthusiasm for these ideas and the anticipation of an exciting year ahead led to many such conversations over the next few weeks, with students and teachers recording their thoughts and preparing for meetings with the head teacher. Almost every student was involved in debating suggestions and making plans; some discussing these with teachers whilst others sought the opinions of their parents. Manju could not recall a time when so many students were united in their commitment to ensuring a range of events that would highlight the importance of the school at the centre of the community. Students at the school were often reminded of the principles of the man after whom the school was named. Dr Ambedkar, whose portrait hung in Mr Desai's office, was a great advocate of education for all and would surely have been pleased with the opportunities afforded to this generation of children in Kalapurum.

Sitting with a group of fellow students on the steps of the school, Manju expressed her thoughts about Dr Ambedkar and the appropriateness of a school named after this great leader who had advocated the encouragement of critical thinking and independence in young people, including those who lived in India's poorest communities.

"Mr Desai was quite right when he said that Dr Ambedkar School is truly a school for all who live in Kalapurum," she declared. "I am sure that my grandparents would have had far more opportunities in their lives if they had been able to attend a school like this."

Manju's fellow students nodded in agreement, recognising that as always, Manju had made a serious observation. Even Bibin who tended to see school as an inconvenient, though necessary passage of time in his life before he could start engaging in far more interesting adult pastimes, had to concede that Manju had made an important point. However, though the majority of students shared Manju's interpretation of the situation, one boy who had sat conspicuously at the edge of their group appeared less impressed with her peroration. Recognising that her fellow student seemed less engaged in the general discussion than might have been expected, Manju got up from her position on the school steps and walked across to sit next to the boy.

"Hi Hari, are you ok?" she inquired.

"Yes, I'm fine," he replied.

"You don't seem to be very keen on the plans being made for the school celebration. Don't you have any ideas you'd like to share?" As soon as she uttered these words Manju could see that her question had made Hari uncomfortable and quickly moved to allay his concerns. "I don't mean to pry, but I know that you are usually full of ideas and I can't understand why you are not joining our conversation." She looked closely at Hari and observed that he was looking down, trying to avoid making eye contact with his classmate.

"Look, I'm just fine. I'll go along with whatever is planned. I just don't want to be part of the conversation at the moment, that's all." With that final short speech Hari got up, turned and walked away, leaving Manju wondering whether she had been right to confront him in this manner. Clearly something was amiss with Hari and his departure left Manju confused and uncomfortable.

3.

The brief conversation that Manju had with Hari troubled her over the next few days. She knew Hari as an intelligent, thoughtful and creative student and had been surprised by his lack of enthusiasm for the plans that were being made. Having pondered this situation and being anxious to ensure that Hari was given every opportunity to be fully engaged in the discussion of ideas, she sought him out one morning before school and checking that they were alone asked him directly. "Why are you so reluctant to discuss the plans for celebrating the twentieth anniversary celebrations?" At first Hari was silent and seemed determined not to discuss the matter, but with a little gentle prompting by Manju he eventually made a hesitant response.

"Mr Desai is right when he says that the school provides opportunities that our parents never had," he began. My father can barely read and write, but I know him to be a clever man. If he had been able to attend Dr Ambedkar School, he would have been a quick learner and would probably have got a good job, a much better life than he has today. That is what he hopes for me. But Mr Desai also said that this is a school for all children and that isn't true. There are children who never get to attend school. I have a sister Priyanka, she doesn't come to school. She stays at home while I attend and get a good education. How can Mr Desai possibly say that this school is for everyone in Kalapurum?"

Manju had heard that Hari had a sister but had never previously thought about why she might not be attending school. Surely, if she was of school age she should be attending like all the other children in Kalapurum. "Why doesn't Priyanka come to school?" she asked. "Mr Desai says that Dr Ambedkar School is for everyone, so why doesn't your sister attend? How can she have been left out?"

Hari shook his head and looked down to the floor, evading Manju's quizzical gaze. "She can't come," he said almost whispering his words. "The teachers won't be able to manage her."

"What do you mean?" Manju asked. "Dr Ambedkar School is for all children. Of course she should come."

"You just don't understand," Hari stated firmly. "Nobody really understands. Priyanka isn't like everyone at this school, she's different."

"What do you mean, different?" Manju enquired. "Why do you say she can't come? Why won't the teachers manage?"

Looking at Hari she detected that he was uncomfortable and possibly on the verge of tears. Perhaps, she thought, I'd better not push this conversation any further. Feeling awkward and anxious that she had been the source of Hari's difficulties she sought reluctantly to change the subject but was immediately interrupted by Hari who turning to face her directly uttered a torrent of words.

"Priyanka can't come to school because she can't walk. She's disabled and can't talk. She has a condition called cerebral palsy. She's always been disabled, ever since she was born. She can't do the things that you and I do, and that means she can't come to school. The school wouldn't want her, and the teachers wouldn't know how to teach her. So, there it is, Dr Ambedkar School is a good school, Mr Desai is a great principal and we are lucky that we have good teachers, but I just know that there is no way Priyanka can attend."

Manju was quiet for a while, unsure how to respond to the information that Hari had never shared with her, or as far as she knew, with any of the other students at the school. Should she have pushed Hari for information in this way, she wondered? She had meant well, but now she could see that she had made him uncomfortable through her persistent questioning and was now uncertain about how to proceed. Eventually, having had little time to assimilate the information provided she decided to take the conversation a little further and tentatively she asked Hari. "Does Mr Desai know you have a sister? Have your parents ever asked about a place at the school for Priyanka?"

Hari shook his head. "What would be the point? How would she even get into the school? She couldn't get up the steps, she uses a wheelchair, and someone needs to push her. And when she got to class, what would she do? She can't hold a pen, she can't answer questions. She isn't stupid, she can understand everything, but she can't do things the way that you and I can. Anyway, if she came to school she would be laughed at by the students, either that or the teachers would pity her. I don't want that for Priyanka. She's my sister and she needs to be cared for, not laughed at."

"But wouldn't you like Priyanka to get an education?" asked Manju. Mr Desai says that Dr Ambedkar believed in education for all, surely that must include your sister. If Priyanka isn't included in school then it isn't a school for all."

Hari was assertive in his response. "A school for all is a great idea, but it isn't real. It means a school for all able-bodied students and those who aren't different. Priyanka isn't like that. Even a good school like ours isn't going to welcome my sister into the classroom. The teachers wouldn't know what to do with her and she would just end up being ignored or laughed at by everyone. It's best that things stay as they are. Now, I don't want to talk about this anymore. "

4.

That evening at home Manju had plenty of time to think about her conversation with Hari. She wondered whether she had done the right thing in pursuing her questioning of Hari. She knew that Dr Ambedkar School had provided her with many opportunities that had been denied to her parents and many others of her generation and recognised how fortunate she was to receive a good education. Her mother had learned to read and write only when she became an adult and found a sympathetic tutor, but her father continued to struggle with anything more than rudimentary text. Priyanka's situation did not seem fair and the discomfort that she had witnessed in Hari made the situation still worse. She felt that it would be almost impossible to change the situation and did not want to embarrass Hari by pursuing matters beyond their private conversation. Perhaps it would be best if she simply left things alone.

The next day during morning break at school Hari approached Manju across the school yard. Before she was able to offer reassurance that she would saying nothing about Priyanka to anyone, Hari took her by the arm and looking around to be sure that they could not be overheard said, "Manju, I just wanted to thank you for listening yesterday. I'm sorry if I seemed angry. I haven't spoken to anyone about Priyanka before but perhaps I should have done. You see, to me she is just my sister. Yes, she is different in many ways, but in lots of others she is just like any other eight-year-old girl. She is intelligent, she likes to laugh, but she is often sad, partly because she can't do the things that I do. Anyway, it was kind of you to listen and to try to understand."

Manju smiled and placed her hand gently on Hari's shoulder. "I am trying to understand," she confirmed. "I won't say anything about your sister to anyone if you don't want me to. But it does seem wrong that Priyanka can't come to school and learn alongside the rest of us. Have you thought about discussing this with Mr Desai? I'm sure he would want to know what you are thinking. He really is committed to making Dr Ambedkar School welcoming to everyone. Perhaps you should speak with him."

Hari shook his head. "What would I say?" he asked. "I can't just tell Mr Desai that my sister should be coming to school, that wouldn't be fair. He does so much for everyone in this community, I wouldn't like him to think that I wasn't grateful. Let's just forget that we ever discussed this shall we? The next year will be a great time for celebrating the school's success, and I wouldn't want to spoil that."

"I can understand why you are worried," said Manju, "but just imagine, there may be other children like Priyanka here in Kalapurum, if not now then in the future. Surely, they should have the right to go the school. Perhaps by talking about this with Mr Desai you could be making a better future not only for Priyanka, but for all children who may in some way be different, don't you think?"

"I have thought about that many times," Hari replied. "And I hope that at some time in the future not just Dr Ambedkar School, but all schools will be open to students like Priyanka. But that will be in the future because schools just aren't ready to accept girls like Priyanka at the moment."

"But it must start somewhere," Manju asserted. "If nobody makes the first move then it will never happen. At least that's what I think. You know more about Priyanka than anyone, so surely you could show everyone here how important it is not to leave her out of school. She needs an education as much as anyone, so perhaps now is a good time to ask for change."

"That all sounds very good," said Hari, "but I can't make things change, who would listen to me?"

"Mr Desai would listen, I'm sure of it," Said Manju with great confidence. "Listen, what is the harm in talking to him. He always listens to what we have to say and if having heard what you can tell him about Priyanka he still can't admit her to the school, well she will not be worse off will she? I think you should talk to him. If you want, I will come with you, but you are the one with the expertise, I can just come to give you support. What do you think?"

Hari thought for a while, then looking at Maju to assure himself that she really was saying what she meant asked, "would you really come with me? If I go to see Mr Desai will you come along with me?"

"Of course, I said I would and I won't let you down, I promise."

5.

On Wednesday afternoon, just after the close of school, Manju and Hari were seated outside the principal's office having made an appointment to see Mr Desai. When the door opened and the principal appeared, he gave his familiar warm smile and welcomed his two students into his room and directed them to sit on chairs at his desk.

"So then, Manju and Hari, I'm always pleased to welcome students into my office, unless of course they have been sent by one of the teachers for some misdemeanour. But I know that this is unlikely with either of you as you are amongst the best of our students. So, tell me, what can I do for you? Have you come with some wonderful idea for next year's celebrations?"

"Well not exactly," began Manju, "though it is related to the things that you said about the importance of celebrating the school and everything it has brought to Kalapurum."

Mr Desai sensed some hesitancy in his student's voice and knowing Manju to be one of his most confident students was intrigued and wondered what it could have been that inspired these two students to visit him in this manner. "Go on," he suggested, "please tell me more about how my words led you to pay me this visit."

Manju looked at Hari and could see that he was shuffling uncomfortably in his chair, a fact that was also discerned by Mr Desai who tried to offer reassurance. "Please, do tell me what is on your mind. If there's a problem and it's anything I can help with I am sure that we can sort things out."

Hari tried to collect his thoughts and to say the words that he had been rehearsing in his mind throughout the day, but the only words he could summons were, "I think Manju can explain better than I can. Please Manju, you know what to say."

Mr Desai recognising Hari's discomposure smiled kindly and sought to put him at his ease. "Alright Hari, I'm sure that whatever it is you want to say Manju can speak for both of you. Let me hear what it is that you want, and I'll see if I can help. So, Manju."

"Right," began Manju, feeling slightly taken aback having rehearsed this meeting several time with Hari over the last couple of days. "Well you see Mr Desai, both Hari and I are very proud of being students at Dr Ambedkar School. We enjoy our lessons and everything about the school and we know how lucky we are to have good teachers, and of course a good principal." She though that she had better add this last clause as a form of insurance. "We are really looking forward to celebrating the twentieth anniversary next year and have been discussing all kinds of ideas. Everyone is very excited at the thought of the coming year and lots of ideas have been discussed. When we heard you speak about the importance of the school and the fact that previously so many people in Kalapurum had not had the chance of an education, it made us realise how lucky we are to be here."

"Well," Mr Desai interjected, "I'm sure that the opportunity to attend school is no more than your right. Every child should attend school. It is not only what Dr Ambedkar advocated, it is also what I believe passionately to be right."

"Yes sir, but that's just it," Manju recommenced her well-rehearsed argument. "Everybody should have the right to attend school, but still not everyone does. Not even here in Kalapurum. You said that Dr Ambedkar School is a school for all children in Kalapurum, but you see it isn't, and that doesn't seem right."

Mr Desai looked directly at Manju with a puzzled expression and said nothing for a minute or so before commenting, "Manju, I'm not quite sure what you mean. I hope that this school makes all children from Kalapurum welcome and I would be most disappointed to think that this was not the case. Please explain what you mean."

Manju took a deep breath and was about to offer a reply when she was interrupted by Hari who suddenly emitted a stream of words that tumbled over one another in their effort to be heard. "It's not your fault sir, it's not anybody's fault really, but it isn't a school for all, not every child can attend. I know that there is nothing that can be done about it, but it's not a school for every child in Kalapurum, it just isn't true and it probably isn't possible."

Mr Desai could see clearly the anxiety on Hari's face and raising a hand tried to take command of the situation. "Slow down, please slow down Hari. I can hardly catch what you are saying. You obviously have some important things you want to tell me and I need to listen to what you are saying. Now please, start again but go much more slowly. I want to hear what you have to say. I think you are suggesting that not all children are welcome at this school and if this is the case, then I want to hear why you think this is the case. So please start again and let me hear what you want to tell me." Mr Desai's voice was soft and reassuring. As he looked at Hari he detected tears in his eyes and was determined not to add to his discomfort.

Manju leaned across to Hari and placing a hand on his assured him of her support." Go on Hari, you can tell Mr Desai far better than I can. Tell him everything you have told me."

Hari looked directly into Manju's eyes and nodded. "Thank you Manju, I'll try."

6.

The following day at lunch time Hari and Manju were called to return to Mr Desai's office. "Please come in and sit down," the kindly principal directed them to chairs. "I have given a lot of thought over night to what you told me yesterday, and firstly can I say Hari how bravely you spoke and how both of you were quite right to come and see me. In fact, I only wish you had come much sooner. You are equally right in your assertions that when I described Dr Ambedkar School as a school for all, I was incorrect. This has left me feeling quite uncomfortable about the words I have used. I was not deliberately stating a falsehood, but none the less I was wrong in making this observation. Not only was I wrong, but I also believe that Dr Ambedkar himself would have been proud of the way in which you brought this to my attention and caused me to consider this situation. He would expect me to address your concerns as a matter of urgency. Until such time as this school can say that it accepts all children from Kalapurum and provides them with a good education, it cannot claim to be a school for all."

Manju and Hari listened carefully to Mr Desai and could see that he was both sincere and troubled by what he had to say. The principal continued. "I cannot pretend that I know all of the solutions. From what you have told me Hari, your sister's needs are many and the school is not well adapted to meet all of these. However, I feel that it must be my responsibility to address this dreadful oversight in denying Priyanka an opportunity to learn. I am sure that this will not be easy, and I know that we will face many challenges, but I have made a decision and whatever the consequences, with your help we will put matters right." Mr Desai nodded his head and smiled looking first at Manju and then at Hari, he continued, "From the first day of the new school year Priyanka will be enrolled in the school. I know that in order to make this happen we will need to confront many difficulties, but we will take our inspiration from Dr Ambedkar who himself faced many prejudices and challenges but was determined to overcome them all. That is what we shall do together. I will need a few days to make a plan and I am appointing you two to be my main assistants in making this plan become a reality. You have both demonstrated the determination to see this through and without you both, and especially without the specific expertise that you have Hari, we are likely to fail. So, I will be relying on both of you to enable Priyanka to not only come to school, but also succeed as a student when she is here. Is this clearly understood?"

Hari and Manju were initially speechless. They could hardly believe what they could hear, but Mr Desai reassured them that Priyanka would indeed be admitted to the school at the start of the new year and that they would be required to play a leading part in ensuring that this happened.

"Now then," concluded Mr Desai. "First things first. This evening Hari I will come home with you to meet Priyanka and to discuss arrangements with your parents. Next week we will meet again and begin to plan for how we make sure that this school becomes a genuine school for all, and to make Dr Ambedkar proud of what we can achieve. I know that this will not be easy, but yesterday I witnessed the great courage that you have Hari and this will be an important inspiration to all of us as we make this work."

As they left the principal's office and made their way towards afternoon lessons, Hari and Manju exchanged glances which betrayed the fact that they were quite overwhelmed by the experience of the meeting with Mr Desai. Whilst feeling proud of their success they also had an overwhelming feeling that the challenges of the next few weeks would be considerable.

7.

If Hari and Manju had felt apprehensive during their initial meeting with the school principal, they were even more anxious a week later as they stood before a gathered assembly of all the teaching staff. Mr Desai had called this meeting with the sole purpose of enabling Hari, with Manju's support, to address all the teachers and explain Priyanka's situation and her needs. Before Hari spoke, Mr Desai explained to the teachers how he had inadvertently misled the school community by using the expression "a school for all". He told of his meetings with Hari and Manju and of his visit to meet Priyanka and her parents. Looking around his staff Mr Desai could see that many of his teachers were unsure about what he was going to ask of them and saw the need to clarify his own thinking on this matter while ensuring that they felt consulted about the decisions that he had made.

"Before we discuss a course of action," he began, "I think it is important that we all listen to what Hari and Manju can teach us about the language that we use. In particular, I think we should consider the description that I made of Dr Ambedkar School as being a school for all. I say this, because Hari, with Manju's support has made me reconsider these words and has assisted me in understanding that I should have been more careful when choosing my words. Furthermore, these two students have given me much to think about in respect of the principles that I have always tried to uphold as an educator. Principles that I have always believed were greatly informed by Dr Ambedkar after whom this school is named." At this point Mr Desai turned towards his two students and with a reassuring smile invited Hari to inform his staff about Priyanka and her needs.

Hari was at first hesitant in his description of his sister. Never before had he, or as far as he knew, any other student been placed in a situation of addressing a gathering of the whole school staff. He began with apprehension, but soon recognised a willingness of the teachers to learn from what he had to say. Many smiled and nodded their heads in a manner that gave him increased confidence and enabled him to speak in detail about Priyanka's needs and also about her abilities, which could so easily be overlooked. What began almost as an ordeal ended with a sense of great relief as Mr Desai made it clear that he had been greatly impressed by Hari's speech and several of the teachers made similar complimentary noises.

Turning to Manju Mr Desai asked her to add her own comments to the gathered assembly. In particular he requested that she should state why she had taken an interest in Hari's sister's situation.

Manju, despite her usual confidence took a few minutes to find her stride. Standing before the teachers she felt that they all looked so much more knowledgeable and authoritative than she was feeling at that moment. However, above all she knew that she had a responsibility to support Hari, and that having come this far, this was no time to hesitate. Manju spoke for no more than five minutes, but in that time the essence of her message was clear to all in the room.

"I know how fortunate I am to come to this school," she began. "When Mr Desai spoke to the whole school and said that many of our parents and grandparents did not have the opportunities to learn that we have, I knew this was true. My father never attended school. He works hard as an auto rickshaw driver, but has often said that he would have liked a different job if he had been able to read and write better than he can today. My mother also missed the opportunity to go to school. She is a very clever lady and only learned to read when she had already started working in the fish market. When Mr Desai said that Dr Ambedkar School is a school for all, I felt very proud and fortunate to be a pupil here. But then when I heard from Hari about his sister, I realised that a school for all did not really mean a school for everybody. Priyanka stays at home and has never been to school and this made me think. What would Dr Ambedkar say about this situation? Many of the children from his community also didn't have an opportunity to attend school, but he did. Dr Ambedkar was a great man who achieved many things. He was the inspiration for this school and I think he would want a school named after him to truly be a school for all. I know that this will be a problem, but I hope that everyone can work together to make this a school that welcomes Priyanka and all children from Kalapurum."

Having concluded her speech, Manju sat down, initially unsure about whether her words had been appropriately chosen, but within a few seconds all of the teachers, led by Mr Desai were applauding and nodding their heads. Hari leaned across to Manju from his chair beside her and thanked her and at this point she felt a great sense of pride and relief.

The acknowledgement of the teaching staff subsided and Mr Desai once more assumed his role as leader of the school community. "I would like to thank Hari and Manju for their excellent presentations," he began. "But now that we have heard from them, and all of us have acknowledged the challenges of truly making Dr Ambedkar School a place that welcomes and teaches all children from Kalapurum, we need to decide how this can be achieved." The teachers before him nodded their agreement and pleased with this response the principal continued. "What I propose is that we should form an action committee comprised of a number of teachers, parents and students. I recommend that this committee should include myself, as principal, Priyanka and Hari's parents, two teachers, Manju and other students and that it should be chaired by Hari, because he has greater expertise about his sister's needs than anyone else currently in this room. I will be asking for teacher volunteers and will address all students when we gather together as a whole school of Friday."

Hari could feel his heart beating faster. The prospect of being on a committee to make such important decisions about the school was certainly daunting, and to be appointed its chairperson even more so. As Mr Desai dismissed the meeting, having rightly anticipated Hari's anxiety he took him to one side and placing his hand on his shoulder reassured him, "Hari, I have every confidence that you will make an excellent chairperson and that with your assistance we will make the necessary changes to this school to enable Priyanka to take her rightful place as a valued student of this school. This is going to be an exciting journey, one through which we will all learn together. This is exactly what a school should be and we will be taking actions of which I am sure Dr Ambedkar would have approved."

Mr Desai's words offered great reassurance, though while he felt proud that the principal placed such confidence in his abilities, he remained apprehensive of what might lie ahead.

8.

The first meeting of what had been named the Dr Ambedkar School Inclusion Committee went even better than Hari and Manju might have hoped it would. Everyone present was committed to making the necessary changes that would enable Priyanka to be admitted to the school and this level of enthusiasm, along with the support provided by Mr Desai, ensured that Hari found his role as chairperson far easier than he had anticipated. As was to be expected, much of the meeting focused upon the many obstacles that seemed to be in the way of Priyanka joining the school. But each time one of these obstructions was presented there were positive suggestions made about how they could be overcome.

By the end of the meeting a plan had been made and a series of actions identified. Mr Desai knew that the community of Kalapurum would be more than willing to assist in putting their plans into practice, and the commitment of everyone present at this and subsequent meetings ensured that progress was quickly made towards making changes to the school environment and the expertise needed by all concerned.

Within two weeks of the initial planning meeting a group of parents, each of whom had experience as builders had met with members of the committee and had quickly made an assessment of where there was a need to install wheelchair friendly ramps, to widen doorways and to make structural changes to the school building that would make it more easily accessible. The greatest challenge from the perspective of these builders would be the provision of a wheelchair accessible toilet. However, after visiting public buildings in Chennai to see examples of such facilities a plan was formulated and the team were convinced that they could provide the necessary changes.

A small group of parents and teachers had been assigned the role of financial planners, and at first they were worried that the proposed building works would be far too expensive for them to achieve. Mr Desai had fewer concerns in this area, advising them that where it was necessary to take actions that would increase the opportunities of those who had been excluded, he was sure that help would arrive. And indeed Mr Desai's prophecy was proven to be correct. As word got around that the school was working to ensure that all children could attend, help came from many directions. A group of local business men agreed that they would fund the costs of building alterations and Kalapurum's largest building company agreed to provide materials and to release some of their workers to complete the necessary alterations.

While the physical changes to the building were taking place, Hari was faced with perhaps his most challenging task to date. At a meeting with Mr Desai, the school principal explained to Hari that there was an understandable apprehension on the part of many teachers with regards to their ability to meet Priyanka's needs. What was needed was a series of training sessions for teachers where they could learn about disability in general and more specifically the ways in which Priyanka could be assisted in school. "I am charging you and Manju with responsibility for organising and delivering this training," Mr Desai stated. "Let me know what I can do to support you, but when it comes to this matter, you have far greater expertise than anyone else in the school. I have arranged for the first session to be held straight after lessons finish next Thursday." Before Hari had an opportunity to question the wisdom of this decision, Mr Desai had risen from his chair and departed his office, leaving his student wondering exactly what he had let himself in for.

Later that day Hari found Manju and told her of his meeting with Mr Desai. Initially she shared Hari's apprehensions, but being essentially an optimist who believed that behind every challenge lay a hidden opportunity, she was soon making suggestions with regards to how they might plan the sessions for teachers. Together they spent the next few evenings together making a plan for the delivery of training, finding some pleasure in the idea that whereas they were normally students, next week they would be instructing their teachers.

9.

Thursday evening soon came around and despite their undoubted enthusiasm, Hari and Manju entered the school hall where all of the teachers including Mr Desai had gathered, with some trepidation. However, they were well prepared and had rehearsed the ways in which they would address the assembly and as the gathered teachers welcomed them with friendly smiles, they gained some confidence. As the teachers settled into their chairs Hari stepped forward and after taking a deep breath began proceedings. "Thank you for gathering here today," he began, "and thank you especially for agreeing to welcome my sister Priyanka to Dr Ambedkar School. Manju and I have been thinking quite hard about the things that you may wish to know that will make it easier for you to teach Priyanka when she arrives. One of the things we decided was that as students ourselves, we often find it easiest to learn when we are asked to do things. Practical activities in lessons help us to understand the things we are taught and therefore today we are going to do a series of practical activities." At this point Hari, having recognised that the teachers were now wondering what they might have to do, turned to Manju and grinned. "Manju will introduce the first of today's activities," he announced and as he did so Manju stepped forward and Hari left through the hall door.

"Don't worry," Manju began. "Hari will return in a few minutes, but it is my pleasure to introduce the first of today's learning activities. Hari and I have called this activity 'getting around'. In order to do this first task we need the help of a professional assistant, someone who has expertise far greater than Hari and I." Manju turned towards the door from which Hari had left and called out "Hari, please bring in our expert teacher."

All eyes turned towards the door and were surprised to see Hari re-emerging pushing a wheelchair in which was seated his sister Priyanka who arrived with a reassuring smile and shouting "hello everyone". As the teachers turned from looking at the new arrivals to question each other, Manju took command ordering everyone to "be quiet please, this is serious lesson and we must all pay attention." At this point Mr Desai nodded and smiled approvingly, ensuring that today's erstwhile teachers would feel comfortable with their new found status.

It was now Hari's turn once more and with renewed confidence he indicated Priyanka saying, "you will already have worked out that this is my sister Priyanka. This is the first time she has been inside the school and I would like to thank you for making her welcome today. Priyanka will be speaking to you all a little later but before then we have two activities planned, the first, as Manju told you, is called 'getting around' and the second we have called 'going for a ride.' Everyone must join in and we hope that you will have fun, because as Mr Desai always tells us, learning is fun. I will introduce the first activity and Manju will explain the second. We will divide you into two groups and after half an hour the two groups will change over so that everyone gets to do both activities."

As Hari was giving his instructions, Manju was walking around the class giving each teacher a card on which was written either a number 1 or a number 2. "Those who have a number 1 card," continued Hari, "will be the first to play 'getting around' and those with a number 2 will play 'going for a ride.' We will then change over after half an hour."

As the teachers examined their cards Hari, who by now was feeling full of confidence, continued to issue his instructions while Manju left the room. "So then, those of you with number 1 will play 'getting around,' to do this activity Manju and I have made a map of the school. It shows both the inside of the building and various locations outside." Hari held up the map in order that everyone present could see. On the map we have identified 10 locations indicated with the letters A to J. At each of these points is a card that contains some information about Priyanka that she has told Manju and I that she would like you to know about her. Your task is to push Priyanka around the course indicated on the map, collecting the cards and reading them aloud. You must change over after each card so that everyone has a turn at pushing Priyanka. If you have any difficulties please remember that Priyanka is an expert in being pushed in a wheelchair. I am sure she will help you with any problems." Looking around the teachers and sensing varying levels of confidence in the task ahead Hari continued to be in charge. "Right, Mr Sinha, you can be first pusher and Mrs Chandra, you can be in charge of the map. Now off you go."

It took a few minutes for the teachers to organise themselves, each being unfamiliar with the situation into which Hari had placed them, but Priyanka soon assisted by greeting everyone in the team and assuring them that she had confidence that they would be quick learners. Recognising that he had been given a task of great responsibility Mr Sinha examined the wheelchair and having located the brake released this and following instruction from Mrs Chandra who directed him towards class 3 the entourage began their journey of discovery.

Those in group 2 awaited further instruction and as soon as the first activity was under way Manju re-entered the hall and began to inform them of the activity that they had chosen to call 'going for a ride'. "In order to complete this activity, we all need to go to the school field, so please follow me," she instructed. The remaining teachers, intrigued as to what lay before them duly followed Manju to the school field, where they were greeted by the sight of a series of cones, ramps and other obstacles laid out as a circuit around the perimeter of the field. Gathering the teachers around her Manju informed them, "to do this activity, Hari and I have had to borrow four wheelchairs from different people in Kalapurum." At this instant Hari drew back a sheet that had been covering the four mentioned vehicles, immediately stimulating the interest of the teachers. "They depend on these chairs to get around and therefore we only have them for this evening's activity" Manju continues. As soon as we finish this evening's lesson we must take them back to their owners".

"When Hari and I talked to Priyanka about the things she felt it was important for you to know, she thought it would be a good idea for you to know what it is like to be pushed around in a wheelchair. So, your task is to take it in turns to either push, or be pushed around the obstacle course. You must weave in and out of the cones, go up and down the slopes and go between the narrow areas we have crated with tables without touching them. It's as simple as that. So off you go."

The teachers quickly organised themselves as Hari went to find out how the first group were managing their task. Before long laughter and chatter could be heard as the groups manoeuvred the chairs around the course, gradually gathering in confidence and proficiency as they proceeded. I think by the sound of things, if Mr Desai is correct, there must be a lot of learning taking place here.

After half an hour Manju and Hari swapped the two groups around so that everyone had the same learning experiences. The teachers appeared more relaxed than at the start of the session and seemed to also be enjoying getting to know Priyanka. At the end of the lesson the young teachers stood before the class and praised them for their participation. "Did you enjoy today's lesson?" asked Hari. The responses of the teachers were wholly positive. "And did you learn anything?" The teachers all began to state things that they had learned, just as they would have expected from their own classes.

Manju stepped forward. "So, now it is time to give you your homework," she announced. Most of the teachers laughed, though some looked a little shocked, not quite sure if they had heard correctly. "There will be another lesson next week and for your homework we want each of you to write down one thing that you learned from this evening's activities and one question that you would like to ask Priyanka. Thank you for being a good class, we look forward to more fun learning next week."

As they were leaving the hall several of the teachers stopped to thank Hari and Manju for the lesson. Almost everyone made a point of speaking with Priyanka as they left, and observing this Manju commented that this had been a most successful evening.

Hari and Manju, ably assisted by Priyanka continued with their weekly lessons for the next five weeks. Each session was made as practical as possible, with lots of activities that included making teaching materials that would be easily accessed by Priyanka, and playing games that helped teachers to understand the challenges that she faced and finding ways to overcome these. But it wasn't only teachers who attended lessons, Hari and Manju organised activities for their fellow students, for school cleaners, Mr Desai's secretary and for those who were working on making the school ready to accept Priyanka on her first day.

While these two students were busy fulfilling their duties as teachers, progress with making changes to the building continued at a pace. In addition to the installation of ramps, modifications to a toilet and widening of doorways, some changes were made in the school library. During their tour of the school with Priyanka in their first lesson with Hari, the teachers had recognised that many of the books and other resources in the school were beyond Priyanka's reach. It would be impossible to move all of the volumes to a lower level, but one of the teachers, Mrs Mahmood had an idea. If we check all of the subject content to be taught to Priyanka's class this year, it would be possible to make sure that related books were placed at an appropriate level that she could reach. Another teacher, Mr Kumar proposed that Priyanka could be allocated a library buddy who could assist her if she had any difficulties accessing books. These suggestions were taken to Hari, Manju and Priyanka for approval. This was immediately given and the teachers noted this as a major success on their path to considering and meeting Priyanka's needs.

By the end of the school term Hari and Manju sensed that confidence across the whole school in respect of enabling Priyanka to enjoy learning alongside her peers had grown. This feeling was shared by Mr Desai who during the final assembly of the school year praised everyone from across the whole Kalapurum community for pulling together to ensure that Dr Ambedkar School would at last become a school for all. During the assembly he drew particular attention to Hari and Manju who had made such an important contribution to achieving this important goal, praising their enthusiasm and determination and stating that along with the other teachers he had learned much from them, and of course from Priyanka.

10.

As was most befitting of such a momentous occasion, the opening of the new school year, one that was to include many events to celebrate the twentieth anniversary of Dr Ambedkar School, was marked with great ceremony. For the first day of the new term the doors of the school were opened to the whole community of Kalapurum and many visitors came to enjoy tours of the school led by students. During the day there were performances by the school choir and dance groups, a recital of poetry from both students and teachers and an exhibition of photographs of the school taken over the course of its first twenty years.

Speeches were made by Mr Desai and by officials from the education office in Chennai who reaffirmed their commitment to ensure that in the future all children in Kalapurum would enjoy the benefits of a good education at Ambedkar School. The mood of the day was one of great joy for everyone, but especially for Priyanka and her parents who looked forward to new opportunities and a much better future than they had previously envisaged.

At the end of the day, as everyone was departing, Mr Desai invited Manju and Hari to his office. "I felt it important," he began, "to see you both and to thank you personally for all that you have done to educate us about what it means to be a school for all. You have been an inspiration to everyone associated with Dr Ambedkar School and indeed to the community of Kalapurum. The work that you have done will ensure that this school continues to play an important role in the lives of all children who live in this district. But I believe that this is probably only the first step on a journey that we must all take together. We have not suddenly all become experts in teaching Priyanka or the many other children who have similarly been excluded from our education system. I have no doubt that the road ahead will have many obstacles and that there will be times when we fail to meet our highest expectations. But the most important thing to remember as we move forward, is that if we work together with great determination and a vision of justice and opportunities for all, we will overcome the challenges and everyone will benefit."

As they left Mr Desai's office at the end of this auspicious day Hari and Manju knew that the principal was correct in his assertion that there would be challenges ahead. They also believed that over the past months they had learned many lessons about the ways in which they could work in the future and that they would maintain their determination to succeed.

Educating Manju

Manju was usually the first to arrive at school each morning, but today was different. Normally she would leave home at 8.30 am. along with her elder brother Bibin, but whilst he generally dawdled and fooled around with other students as they met them along the road, Manju would hurry ahead, keen to be early at the school gates. Today however, Manju was in no hurry to arrive. This was no ordinary day and she left home with mixed emotions and too many thoughts playing on her mind.

Dr. Ambedkar Government School was only twenty minutes' walk from the small house where Bibin and Manju lived with their parents. Perhaps a little longer on a busy day, when it could take a while to cross the main road and to dodge between the constant flow of traffic. In all her days as a student Manju had never once been late and whilst today would be no different in this regard, she somehow felt less anxious than she would normally have been about arriving before the morning bell was sounded. It wasn't that she didn't care. In fact it could be said that this was less a change of attitude and more to do with her current state of confusion.

Along with many friends who lived in her block, Manju had started at the primary school when she was six years old. From day one she had relished the opportunity to learn and quickly understood that school was exactly where she wanted to be. Whilst she would never have said that learning came easily to her, Manju found that she could respond well to the new challenges which came her way. She quickly learned that through determination and hard work she could achieve marks that were as good as those of anyone in her class. Though at first she had assumed that she was not as clever as others in the class, she soon realised that this was simply a matter of learning how to think in English rather than turning over every idea in Tamil before responding to the teacher's demands. Within a year of starting school Manju was being regularly praised by her teacher for the consistency of her work across all subjects, and then she knew that this was exactly where she wanted to be.

Hard work, achievement and recognition by her teachers; this had been the pattern of Manju's school life for the past six years. Over this time she had received many accolades and had three times won the end of year prize given to the best performing student. The school principal Mr Desai had singled her out as an outstanding scholar, a student who in his estimation would go far and make the whole community proud. When visitors came to the school it was often Manju who was asked to stand and read aloud from an essay that she had recently composed. Yet, despite all this praise Manju kept her feet on the ground. She knew that to reach the levels that she had attained had involved hard work and commitment well above that which other students appeared to be prepared to make. But she also realised that she was treading a precarious path and that whilst her teachers saw for her a bright future, other influences in her life were less auspicious.

The conversation that Manju had had with her parents a month ago had not been easy for any of them. Manju loved her father and knew that he loved her too. He was invariably kind and attentive; often playful with her and willing to give her time. But Manju also realised that life was hard for her family and that money was far from plentiful. Her father's job as an auto rickshaw driver was more secure than that of some of her friends' parents, but the income to be gained was never fully assured and he often worked long into the night. Manju's mother was similarly hard working as a homemaker who took pride in the appearance of her children as she saw them off to school each day. She herself had never had such an opportunity and to see Bibin and Manju leaving home in their neatly pressed school uniforms was a source of great satisfaction.

Manju observed the way in which her mother looked around at their neighbours as she and her brother left home each day for school.

She knew that she sought the affirmation and respect that would come from the expressions of the women who watched, as she and Bibin began their morning journey to the school. Though the words were never spoken, Manju's mother was keen to see that these other women knew that her children were being raised to shine. Manju, knowing the sacrifices that her parents made on behalf of Bibin and herself felt that her mother's occasional periods of self-pride were more than justified.

Today however, everything seemed to be out of kilter and Manju found herself dawdling to school and reflecting on how much had changed in the course of a few weeks. Knowing the sacrifices her parents had given just to see her leave for school each day had not made the conversation which she had with them on that fateful Sunday evening a month ago any easier. She understood from the moment she was summoned by her father that a serious discourse was about to follow. The tone of his call and a slight hesitation as he shaped his words were enough to give her cause to be particularly attentive. Sitting before him on the floor she noted how he glanced uncomfortably in the direction of her mother whose own expression was hidden as she stood silhouetted by the bright sunlight that surrounded her as she leant in the doorway.

The conversation began as many whose real purpose is difficult to manage do, with plenty of platitudes and soft words. Taking her hand in his, Manju's father told her how proud both he and her mother were of her many achievements and that she made them happy in everything she did. He smiled awkwardly as he gently squeezed her hand ensuring that he had her full attention. Immediately Manju understood that the messages to be heard were not going to be to her liking. She had heard such opening gambits before and knew that they generally presaged something less palatable.

"Just look at you", her father began. "Such a fine young lady. Whatever became of the little girl we had? It seems like only yesterday I was bouncing you on my knee." Manju didn't know what to say, or even if she was expected to respond at all. Manju's father made another quick glance towards her mother before continuing to speak. "Well now Manju, you are no longer a child. You have grown into a fine young woman, one to make all of us proud and that's for sure." He looked directly into Manju's eyes, trying to gauge any indication that she might have anticipated the message he was about to convey. Seeing nothing that would help him he frowned and wondered if he should perhaps adopt a more direct approach. Still receiving no reaction from his daughter he took the decision and went straight to the point. "Your mother and I, well we've been doing a lot of thinking of late. As you know things are not always easy for us and sometimes we have to make difficult decisions about the future." He hesitated slightly before continuing, looking again for clues in his daughter's eyes, but finding that they were not there. "The truth of the matter is", he stated, though with little real conviction in his voice, "the truth of the matter is that the time has come when we feel that it would be best for you to finish at the school".

For the first time since this conversation began Manju's father saw the reaction he had feared from his daughter. Having anticipated exactly the expression that he now saw upon her face he hurriedly continued with his argument before she could add her own voice to the conversation. "As, I say, we are both so proud of what you have done at school. We know that you have been a hard working student and have learned so much. But now you are no longer a child, you are a young woman and the time has come for you to take on new responsibilities in the home." He wanted to continue without interruption, but before he could do so Manju broke her silence with an anguished cry.

"No, please father no. You can't. I mustn't leave school I still have so much to do. You yourself say I am a good student. Mr Desai and my teachers say I am doing well. Please, I beg of you father, please don't make me leave."

Manju's father had anticipated a reaction, but the vehemence of his daughter's reply took him by surprise. In response he tried desperately to adopt a placatory tone which he hoped would soften the blow. "Please Manju; it's not that we don't know that you have been a good student. As I say we are both so proud of what you have done. We know that you have worked hard at your school books. Every report we have had from the school has been good. But you must surely realise that there comes a time when girls must turn their attention to the important learning, which they need to be good homemakers and to prepare for the life that awaits them".

If he really thought that Manju would be pacified by offering this gentle form of reasoning, Manju's father was soon disabused. Far from appeasing his daughter he immediately realised that his line of argument had quite the opposite effect.

In anger Manju shouted, "If my school work is so good and the reports from school are so positive then why will you not let me continue with my studies? Can you not see that If I study hard I can make you even more proud? Perhaps in a few years' time I could become a teacher, or even a doctor or a lawyer. Can't you see how important this is to me? Manju found herself shaking and felt tears dampening her eyes. "How could you, how can you treat me like this?" She shook her hand free from her father's grasp and stood as if to leave the room.

For the first time since this conversation began, Manju's mother intervened, as pushing forward from the doorway she took Manju by the shoulders. "Listen Manju," she began in tones that were far firmer than those heard up to this point. "You were the first girl in our family to go to school. Girls in this community have never had the opportunities you have had. We have treated you very fairly. You must listen to your father. He has made a decision and it for your own good and for that of all the family. You have done well at school but now the time is right. You are no longer a child and it is time to think of what it means to be a woman in this community. Soon you will be old enough to marry and no man will want you unless you can show that you can manage a home. The time has come to put your childhood behind you and to close your school books in order to begin the learning which you need for the real world."

As often happens in the heat of the moment Manju could no longer think clearly. Later she could vaguely recollect some of her shouted responses, but even of these she was not totally sure. "It's just not fair", was an expression she was sure she had used several times. "Why should Bibin stay on at school when he hates it so much, but then you make me leave?" This part of her rant, for that was clearly what it had become, was certainly true, though it did little to help her cause. If she understood matters correctly, the only argument for Bibin's continuation in education was simply that he was a boy and not a girl. Where, she wondered was the logic, let alone the justice in this statement.

Inevitably the conversation ended badly with Manju confined to her room, told that she should never defy her father, she had shown little gratitude for the opportunities she had been given, that she had disappointed her mother with her attitude and that the matter was at a close. A decision had been made, it was final and there would be no more discussion about the matter. And so it was that the debate reached it's far less than satisfactory conclusion.

So it was that a decision had been reached and now, this was to be Manju's last day at school. The urgency with which she had taken the route to the school gates each day was no longer there. She would not be late, but why should she hurry? For other students this was simply the last day of the school year with a long and welcome break from studies on the near horizon, but for Manju, as far as she was concerned this might as well be the last day of her treasured existence. As she entered through the school gates she found herself making an effort to hold back tears. When her many friends greeted her she contrived a smile but found it almost impossible to return their salutations.

The school bell rang and minutes later Manju found herself in a familiar position seated at her desk. On the surface this, her final day of formal education, progressed in much the same manner as the many hundreds that had preceded it. Mathematics, Hindi and English lessons passed uneventfully, though even in the history lesson, usually her favourite subject, Manju found it difficult to demonstrate much by the way of enthusiasm. Many of her classmates were happy that this was the final day of term and that for a few weeks they would be free from what they saw as the constraints of the classroom, but Manju felt unable to share their enthusiasm. If they were so keen to be away from here, why then might they not swap places with her? She so desperately wanted exactly those things that they seemed to value so little. As far as Manju was concerned there was no justice in this world.

The morning's lessons passed and at lunchtime Manju took up her usual position on the stone bench beneath the large bean tree that afforded welcome shelter from the glare of the sun. She opened her lunchbox as she did every day and examined the food which her mother had carefully prepared. Today she noted there were extra portions of mango, her favourite fruit. This Manju took to be a clear indication that her mother recognised the sadness that she would be feeling at this point in her final day at school. Whilst some of the anger which Manju had felt towards her parents in the weeks immediately following the decision to withdrawal her from school had dissipated, she found herself unmoved by this motherly gesture of appeasement. She would not be so easily pacified. Perhaps, she thought, I am being unkind, but even if this was the case she was unprepared to accept that the decisions made were in her own interest.

Several of Manju's classmates came to sit beside her at the start of that break time. They knew that this was a difficult day for their friend and most were sympathetic to her plight, even though some would happily have exchanged places with her in order to escape from what they saw as the drudgery of school. Many had offered condolences as they might have done had their friend been experiencing bereavement, and indeed this seemed appropriate on one level as Manju contemplated what was for her, a tragic loss. The kindly gestures that they now made, offering small delicacies from their own lunchboxes, placing a consoling arm around her shoulder, were well meant but served only to emphasise to Manju the injustices that she knew she must face alone.

A few minutes had passed since the start of the break time when Manju became aware of another presence having arrived beneath the tree. Looking up she realised that she had been unexpectedly joined by the school principal, Mr Desai. As he began to settle himself on the bench beside Manju, many of her friends moved away, sensing that that the principal's presence there was focused upon Manju and that their attendance may not be necessary or even welcomed. A few hovered just close enough to be sure to hear any conversation that might pass between the two central figures in this scene.

For a while Mr Desai sat in silence and Manju, unsure of how to respond to this unexpected presence did likewise. After a few minutes however, the principal, having seemingly collected his thoughts turned his attention to his student. "Manju," he began, "today is an important new beginning for both of us. Today, like you when I pass through the gates of Dr. Ambedkar School it will be for the last time." He paused briefly before continuing. "Unlike you, I will be leaving after a long time of working within its classrooms, firstly as a teacher and more lately as the principal. But now I am tired and getting old and unlike you, I have made up my own mind about leaving." Manju looked up at Mr Desai and tried to search for any emotion which might have been revealed in his face, but could discern nothing. Neither sadness nor relief were in evidence there and she was unsure why he had come to find her in this way. She wanted to tell him how she was feeling at that precise moment. She wanted him to know that she was struggling to behave like the fine young woman that her father had seen her to be, when really she wanted to cry like the unhappy young girl that she knew herself still to be. But neither words nor tears would come. All she could do was sit in silence and accept her fate without protest.

Mr Desai gave no indication of either his own emotions or of any understanding of what might be going through Manju's mind. "I just thought," he said. "That I would come and say goodbye to a young lady who I know will continue to be a good student for the rest of her life. In a few days' time I will be returning to my old family home in Madurai, but I have many friends here and from time to time they will report to me about the progress which I know you will continue to make." With this promise Mr Desai rose from the bench and before Manju could collect her thoughts and make a reply he was walking away from her, back towards the school building.

This strange encounter with Mr Desai occupied Maju's thoughts throughout the afternoon sessions in class. Why she wondered had he singled her out in this manner? What did he mean about watching her future progress? These questions danced around her thoughts whilst what was left of her last day at school drew towards a close.

The final ritual of the school year was an assembly of all the school's students gathered in the compound in front of the main school entrance. This event had followed the same format each year since she had been enrolled as a student, with Mr Desai presenting a review of the school's academic, cultural and sporting successes, singling out individual students for particular praise and finally awarding prizes to the male and female students of the year. At just such an event Manju had on three occasions been the recipient of that very prize which always took the form of framed certificate and medallion on a ribbon in the school colours placed around the neck of the star student by the school principal.

As in previous years Mr Desai lauded the achievements of specific students and praised the performances of the girls' volleyball and boys' basketball teams and a recent fine performance by the school choir. The climax of the gathering came with the awarding of the prize for the year's outstanding students. On previous occasions Manju had listened to this part of the proceedings with her fingers crossed, hoping that her efforts might have been recognised. This year the announcement seemed of little consequence. When therefore the name of Anjana Prasad was called to receive the girl's award, Manju showed little emotion. She applauded Anjana's success as was only right, but knew that at this, the final moment of her days at Dr Ambedkar School, her association with such rituals was coming to an end. As Mr Desai dismissed his students, wishing them all a good break from their studies, Manju suddenly realised that he had not once mentioned that he too would be leaving the school. Perhaps, she thought, he sees his own departure as being inconsequential and maybe he won't miss the place. If this was the case then his emotions were far removed from those which she herself was experiencing at that moment.

Walking away from the school that evening Manju did not look back. If her school days were over she thought, then I will put them behind me. Bibin walked home beside her, for once neglecting to join his friends. He could sense the sorrow in his sister and felt that at this time, as Manju's big brother, he should show himself to be supportive. They walked together in silence, neither of them having an understanding of the kind of words that might have been appropriate at this time. The journey home was uneventful, each of them seemingly alone with their thoughts, but as they approached their house they could see their mother awaiting them and as they drew near she shouted excitedly. "Manju, Manju, come quick you have a parcel here. Come quickly and see."

Bibin quickened his pace, curious to see what this mysterious parcel for his sister could be, but Manju continued at her steady pace, even this announcement failing to raise her enthusiasm. However, as she reached the threshold of the house her mother eagerly thrust into her hands a brown paper parcel which had been left beside the door earlier in the day. "Quickly, open it Manju, let's see what it is" demanded

Bibin, who could not recall a previous time when a parcel had been delivered to their house.

Manju took the parcel from her mother and examined it carefully. There, written clearly on the brown paper was her name, for the attention of Miss Manju Sudev. There could be no doubt, the package was intended for her and on any occasion other than this she would undoubtedly have shown her excitement. Bibin and Manju's mother looked on as Manju turned the parcel over in her hands, impatient for her to reveal the contents. Having toyed with the object for several minutes Manju looked towards her mother. "Who brought this?" see demanded, "when did it come?" "I don't know" replied her mother, "when I returned from the market this afternoon, there it was beside the door. Aren't you going to open it?"

Manju took a few steps away from the house and seated herself on a low wall. Having turned the parcel over several times in her hand she carefully began to peel away the brown paper to reveal the contents. Slowly, as the paper was removed, she was able to see that the parcel contained a book and there also, concealing the front cover of the book, a long white envelope which again bore her name.

Carefully putting the book and packaging aside without further examination, she took the envelope and tearing open the gummed flap removed a letter which she spread across her lap before taking it up and reading it silently to herself.

Dear Manju,

Today marks the beginning of a new phase in our education as we say goodbye to Dr Ambedkar School, a place which has been very important for both of us. Please note that I say that this is a new beginning and not an ending.

Education has always been significant in my life, as both a student and a teacher. It will continue to be just as important as I move to Madurai to take up new challenges and exciting learning opportunities. For although I will be officially retiring, I am planning to learn many new things. I have decided, for instance that I am going to learn the names and habits of all the birds, the butterflies and the trees in the area where I will live. I have always wanted to do this, but was never able to do so until now because my duties at school gave me so little time. I also intend to read and learn by heart the poetry of Tagore which I knew as a young man but have since largely forgotten.

I say that Dr Ambedkar School has been important for both of us, and this I believe to be true. But for each of us the school could only provide a small part of our education. We have been lucky indeed to have the opportunity which comes from formal schooling. But never doubt that attending school and being educated are not the same thing. School has provided the foundations for your learning, now you must build upon these.

I know that at present you probably find it hard to see education in terms other than those associated with attending school, but please open your mind to the learning that awaits you.

Look at the fishermen who live in your community. They can go many miles out to sea and catch fish. They navigate their way far from land. They can read the weather. They can feed their families. These are educated men, who may never have been to school, but they have learning such as you and I can hardly imagine.

Think about the vegetable sellers who everyday load their barrows and make such beautiful displays at the market near where you live. They understand their customers and work hard to serve their community on the basis of what they have learned and understand. These too are educated people who know so many things that I cannot hope to comprehend, though their learning has not come from books.

Manju. You are one of the brightest students who I have ever had the pleasure to teach. I know that you will continue your education both through your continued reading and thinking about the wider world, and by learning to understand the contribution which you can make to your community. I therefore hope that you will both enjoy and learn from the book which I am pleased to gift to you today, but also from the work which you do for your family and those who you see in need around you.

Today marks the beginning of the next stage of your education. I believe that you will make the most of the opportunities for learning that await you.

I will look forward to following your progress in the coming years as you become an ever more educated person.

Yours sincerely

V.J. Desai

Manju realised that she had tears in her eyes for the first time today, but that she no longer felt sad. She carefully refolded the letter and replaced it in the envelope, knowing that she would read it again many times. Reaching down she picked up the book that lay beside her and examined it carefully beginning with the title "The Story of My Experiments with Truth" by M.K. Gandhi.

"Well Manju, what is it?" asked her mother.

"Homework," she replied with a smile, as she got up and took the book and the letter to her room to begin what she now hoped would be the next phase of her education.

Part Two

OBSERVATIONS AND OPINIONS

ESSAYS AND SHORTER PIECES

A Guest in Poonthura

A teacher who establishes rapport with the taught, becomes one with them, learns more from them than he teaches them. He who learns nothing from his disciples is, in my opinion, worthless. Whenever I talk with someone I learn from him. I take from him more than I give him. In this way, a true teacher regards himself as a student of his students. If you will teach your pupils with this attitude, you will benefit much from them.

Mohandas Karamchand Gandhi (1869 – 1948)

(Talk to Khadi Vidyalaya Students, Sevagram Ashram, 15 February 1942)

Morning

Morning breaks early. The azaan call of the Muezzin brings the mosque nearer than I had thought it to be. I find myself wondering is this an actual man or simply a recording as might be heard from the minarets of many English cities. The rising and falling of the call to prayer is a catalyst for a confusion of sounds both near and in the middle distance. Allâhu ¾akbar elicits a bleating response from goats in the next-door compound and a crowing cockerel from across the road. Allâhu ¾akbar reverberates from distant walls and echoes around the streets. Allâhu ¾akbar and Jament is stirring on the veranda, I hear him shuffling across the dusty concrete floor, rustling papers, clearing his lungs and beginning his daybreak routine.

On the roof above my bedroom crows are careering madly across the terracotta tiles, from my supine vantage they sound much heavier than they are, punctuating their dance with occasional raucous and argumentative calls. In the distance I hear voices, softly spoken and indistinct tones of Malayalam which I gauge to be along the road towards the river. The house is small and I am aware of soft breathing from adjacent rooms seemingly undisturbed by the orchestration of the morning. To others in this home the sounds that engage my curiosity are too familiar to warrant more than a turning over on a mattress.

The muezzin has ceased his call and I stir myself somewhat reluctantly, shifting the mosquito net in order to leave the comfort of the bed. As I rise, swinging my feet to the warming floor a wall lizard scurries to the eves, disappearing between the topmost bricks and the tiles. Why, I wonder does this scuttling action invariably take me by surprise despite a familiarity with the habits of these creatures that goes back years? I hold the comforting thought that lizards feed on mosquitos those constant irritants of the night.

It is early morning in Poonthura and the temperature suits me well. Later it will be hot for sure, but for this moment I bathe in the warmth as I stretch my limbs in readiness for the day ahead. Pulling back the curtain across the bedroom doorway I meet Jament and an exchange of smiles compensates for our mutual linguistic inadequacies. I feel welcomed and at ease in a home that is so different from my own. Standing on the veranda, blinking in the brilliance of the early sunlight I take in the air and savour the scent of spices and dry warm earth that is uniquely India.

Assailed with continuous motion, sound and bright colours the guest in Poonthura like a child in a sweetshop barely knows where first to cast his eyes. Off the main street the alleys and passageways wind in a disorientating maze, each corner turned revealing new sensations and setting the mind racing in an effort to understand. Each building encountered is unique – individual in design and structure, personalised and shaped to fit its inhabitants. Here, walls of thatch take their station alongside others more robust in concrete or brick. Terracotta tiled sloping roofs abut others of corrugated iron creating a crazy geometry above the twisting lanes. And everywhere a tangle of wires and cables seemingly festooned from posts and walls like the tentacles of some strange creature that has emerged with time – surely such an array could never have been planned this way.

Throughout the village small shops, their frontage open to the streets draw their customers in with vivid displays of coloured packages and plastic jars stuffed full of wares. The shutters flung wide bearing Malayalam posters advertising 3G technology alongside catholic imagery of Christ and the Virgin Mary. Hidden in the shadows deep inside each tiny emporium the vendor sits patiently awaiting customers. Sweet smells draws the visitor to the fresh and succulent fare of the fruit and vegetable shop, as fine a greengrocer as could be found in any English high street. Bananas in shades from green to red, okra, onions, tomatoes, brinjals, jackfruit and a range of spices in a vivid display neatly arranged in boxes and trays.

In the morning, following their toil the fishermen arrive trudging weary from their labours, purchasing betel leaf and other associated paraphernalia which they take away wrapped in newspaper as they return to the beach to gain some solace and leisure with their companions. Sagacious men and bold young pretenders gather in circles to exchange news of the past few hours during which they have toiled to provide for their families, just as did their forefathers back through the sea-spume of time for longer than it is possible to imagine.

In the village the traffic is thankfully easier to negotiate, though no less orderly than in Indian cities. The ubiquitous auto rickshaw dominates as the chief form of transport for man and goods. Regular buses come and go from the open ground beside St Thomas' church and motorbike riders weave their way through pedestrians, dogs and the ever present crows. Men and boys on bicycles arrive at shops and houses, parking them on stands, no locks required and confident that they will be there when they return. And then of course the magnificent painted lorries, those veritable art galleries of the road. A driver slows as he sees me taking a photograph, rightly proud of his mighty juggernaut and pleased that it will be captured and shared with others. Individual in their designs and masters of the road, these beasts are at the head of the traffic food chain on India's roads. "Sound horn," but be sure to get out of the way!

Religious symbolism is everywhere in the village, vying for attention alongside communist party propaganda signified by hammers and sickles such as might have been seen in eastern European cities twenty years ago. The church, the mosque or the temple dominate the lives of many of Poonthura's citizens taking their dues and more, and offering a focal point for life's rites of passage. St Thomas' church with its domineering tower holds its place of prominence at the heart of the village, whilst the magnificent mosque and the brightly painted temple have been pushed nearer to the edges. The sounds of familiar hymns sung in a strange language can sometimes be heard escaping the church as one passes. Charles Wesley and Henry Alford translated into Malayalam, just as they would have wished. The call to prayer competes with Christian singing in the morning, whilst the temple appears to have adopted a much quieter, almost understated approach. Here the Hindu worshipers enter between garish figures, buxom painted temple dancers adorn the pillars of a portico whilst in the temple compound Lord Krishna wrapped in garlands summonses the devout with music from his flute.

The area around the path leading to the beach is dominated by a shanty town of huts and lean-to buildings, a hub for fishermen and all the accoutrements of their trade. Here, at the edge of the village the sea takes centre stage. Green breakers crested with silver foam his and spit as they rush their way across the gritty strand. Walking away from the bustling village streets one is immediately aware of the dominance of the ocean and the vulnerability of a people living at its edge. "Before the tsunami," I am told, "the beach was much deeper and the sea much further away". Is it fatalism or blind faith that encourages the villagers to think that it could never happen again, or at least, not here? This is the domain of hard working men. This is no beach for idling away the time or sitting in the sun, this is the working heart of Poonthura. The village and community in which I have been made welcome feels comfortable now, but underneath the slow moving life of the villagers lurks a frisson based upon uncertainty about the future. Life here, for all its colour and apparent ambling pace is far from easy for the inhabitants of Poonthura.

The Village streets – People

Outside the temperature is thirty three degrees and it is humid, but seated on the floor in Moses' woven and thatched house it is cool. Drinking chai in the semi-darkness, our talk is about the village but mostly about Moses' forthcoming marriage. He has been Johnson's friend since school days, and like him he has pursued a formal education which may ultimately see him assume a position of influence within the village or beyond. Therein is a conundrum. What is there to keep young men like Moses or Johnson in the village? Now that they have seen beyond the horizon will they want to stay and work for their community? If the fishing continues to decline and more young people seek lives outside the village what will be the future for Poonthura? People here live hard and simple lives and utilise their space with efficiency. The room in which we sit serves as both a living space and with the careful placement of a desk and chair doubles as Moses' study and office. It is this premium of space and its multi-functional usage that is apparent everywhere within Poonthura.

The progress made when walking the streets of Poonthura with Johnson is inevitably slow. Like a celebrity everyone wants to speak with him, to catch up on the news. "How long are you back in the village for? Are you still studying in England?" and probably "who's the stranger you've brought to the village?" Within a short distance of our walk I appear to have made a hundred new friends. Curiosity inevitably prevails. Ladies smile and namaskar, accompanying their greeting with that familiar south Indian shake of the head. Johnson's male friends, after checking my credentials with him shake me firmly by the hand. All seem genuinely interested and want to pass some time in discussion. People here have time for each other and enjoy every opportunity to engage in casual conversation. Passing the time of day is an expectation and to hurry on without a word would be a social blunder. "Velakarin, velakarin" (white man) children shout, with the uninhibited approach that children the world over display. The braver amongst them test out their English. "Name is?" appears to be the usual opening gambit. "My name is Richard," I reply, "what's your name?" Some answer but most simply shake their heads and smile. Satisfied at having gained a response they run off laughing to share their information with their friends.

At the market squatting women sell bark and driftwood fuel for fires. Others guard small piles of vegetables, onions, brinjals and an assortment of multi-coloured gourds. A chattering group sit with piles of coconuts and jackfruit. A lady slices into a fruit displaying its luscious yellow and cream centre to attract her customers, urging them to buy. She shouts something to me, winks and laughs, knowing that I don't understand. I smile in return and she nudges her neighbour passing some comment, which she knows I cannot comprehend.

The market is buzzing with conversation as women laugh and argue their way from one vendor to the next. The talk appears every bit as important as the sale and the impression is given that this is as much a social gathering as a place for trade. Another woman arranges fish, no bigger than the whitebait served in restaurants at home, on an upturned wooden box. She has brought her entire wares in two aluminium bowls and has set up her makeshift stall in the centre of the market. She is comfortable here and fits easily into the bustle of the place. Such communities are shaped by the familiar bodies that have inhabited them for centuries and I can easily imagine the stranger from two hundred years ago would have witnessed scenes similar to these which capture me today. This is the fisher woman's domain, a familiar routine, somewhat like a ritual that has been played out over many years and no longer needs rehearsal. Her place is assured and she forms one part of the important fabric of Poonthura market place.

At the temple we are greeted by a swami whose interest in us is matched by my own curiosity about him. His matted hair hanging well beneath his waist and his long curled fingernails would draw comments about neglect at home. Here they are accepted as an indication of his aesthetic lifestyle and devotion to his faith. His intelligent eyes shine as he appears to examine my every detail. Johnson explains who I am and he nods as if to say "just as I thought?" "Have you been in Poonthura long?" I ask through Johnson. He tells me that he was sent here some years ago by his guru in the north, that he has travelled across India and visited many places. He has been to the holy Ganga at Varanasi and has seen the Himalayas. He is here because of Swamigal the wandering avadoot who settled here in Poonthura and is revered by devotees. He indicates the statue of Krishna and other features of the temple and appears pleased that we are interested in what he has to show, but then seemingly loses interest and leaves us without any formality or comment.

As we leave the temple a group of boys leave off from their game of cricket, calling to Johnson to know who the stranger is he's brought. After a moment's conversation a young sportsman approaches me and offers the bat. Johnson grins and I march purposefully to take my place at the imaginary crease. Five balls faced and I am feeling well set. A leg glance of sorts to the boundary has raised my aspirations. Confidence inevitably leads to my down fall as the sixth delivery, I swear it turned a foot, finds a leading edge and a simple return catch to the bowler signals the end of a brief innings. My nemesis smiles and I return the bat offering thanks for the opportunity given to revisit my youth. "He wants to know if he bowls well," Johnson says. "Tell him he's a rising star and that I hope to see him in a test match at Lord's someday," I say. The lad is pleased with that and returns to the game to terrorise the next unsuspecting batsman.

The pace of the outside world has to an extent left Poonthura behind. I seem to remember from my own childhood a time when men would stand at street corners and pass the time of day. As a child, cricket in the streets with stumps chalked upon a wall was played on long summer days and in the evenings well beyond a time when the light was adequate for a clear sighting of the ball. The sense of community that is still present in Poonthura is a precious gift which is more than worthy of preservation. For the inhabitants of this ramshackle village it passes as unexceptional, simply because it is the norm and most have always accepted that it is this way. Inevitably modernity has entered the lives of the people of Poonthura and much of this is for the best. It is perhaps too much to hope that with the coming changes this sense of comfortable belonging will remain.

Fishermen

One man calls and the others respond. The rhythmic chant typical of those associated with labour and particularly the hauling of ropes and nets throughout the world, aids the muscular efforts of satchel skinned men.

If 'work is worship' then these men sacrifice themselves daily through their physical exertions in pursuit of an uncertain return and the hope that today's catch may be better than the last. Sinews strain as each man, digging his heels deep in the sand levers from the knee and bows his back to the task. The net advances only slowly, but the tempo of the men's endeavours ensures a gradual advance heaving the heavy mesh nearer to the shore. Beneath each cloth-bound head the exertions of the men are etched in their faces; sweat glowing on cheeks tensed and grimaced with the strain.

An anchor man systematically and skilfully coils the incoming net, the pile behind him gradually growing higher, measuring the progress of the haulers. As each man reaches the anchor point he peels off from the line returning slowly, stooped from his endeavours to the front of the team, repositioning himself and recommencing his work. There is little respite here. These are hardened men inured not in a job, but in a way of life; for the very lifeblood of Poonthura is dependent on their labours. Theirs is an unheralded dignity, one built upon a cohesion born not out of an orderly team selection, but rather from necessity. There are no appointed leaders here. Each man plays his role; none requires direction as each has lent his efforts to the task in the same way for generations. Along the line are young men and old who heave with calloused chafing hands along the ropes, each contributing to the physical enterprise from an inheritance of toil passed down from father to son. The lore of the fishing is ingrained in each strained sinew of their muscular bodies.

As the net approaches the shore the excitement mounts and with it the volume of the chanting and urgent calls. The swimmers first seen as mere dots on the ocean carefully guiding the net have come ashore and now shout their encouragement to the haulers. Gradually the net is closed, cries from the men in the sea increase the anticipation. "They seem to think it's a good catch" Johnson tells me. The anticipation is palpable; the atmosphere has shifted from one of ordered rhythmic motion to a much more frantic effort to make the final hard won yards. There are more men in the sea now, reaching and hauling on the final yardage of the net. The force of the waves knocks mere men from their feet, the surf crashing against them before its power dissipates on the sand.

From along the beach towards the village gangs of women appear, many carrying large round bowls upon their heads. Their excited banter can be heard long before they arrive. Soon they will be here for the spoils. The gathering is joined by flocks of snow-white herons anticipating a possible spill from the catch. They keep a safe distance, knowing that their intended theft will not find favour with the assembled villagers.

Gradually the catch appears. First in singles, writhing, twisting, catching morning sunlight, caught in the salt-sea weeping ,tangled netting as it emerges from the surf, then in greater numbers until a final heave delivers the bulk of the catch, silver squirming, flashing like shattered fragments of mirrors amidst the netting on the beach. Straightening their creaking bodies after their morning exertions the fishermen encircle their quarry, staring hard at the gasping catch. Disappointment can be read in many of their faces. The anticipated bounty has not materialised. The catch is poor and offers such a small return for so great an effort. Whilst some of the men look on in resignation others vent their disappointment in quarrels, seeking to justify the efforts of the morning through an analysis of what might have been. "What are they saying?" I ask, "We should have done this differently", says Johnson. They make suggestions and look for reasons for their poor return. Some men simply turn away. They have seen this all before. Maybe they recognise a pattern here. Perhaps the older men, those who have seen far better days are resigning themselves to an understanding that the days of plenty are unlikely to return.

Scooping the silver fish into their bowls the women join the dispute with greater vigour than the men whose energy is largely spent. Shaking of fists and pointing of fingers become the order of the morning in a scene that I suspect is oft repeated on this stretch of shore. Here is an anger founded on frustration and anxiety. Fishing, for so long the heartbeat of Poonthura no long provides an assurance of the subsistence, which is all these proud people crave. Uncertainty breeds mistrust and with it comes rage. The fishermen look on; but whilst they appreciate the causes of dispute many appear too exhausted to continue the debate and leave it for the women to resolve. They know that in truth there is no resolution. Several of the fishermen take replenishment through the chewing of betel leaves as they disperse into smaller groups and attempt to justify the poor return for their endeavours. Others turn their attention to the management of the nets, preparing them once more for what they hope will next time be a better day.

I am sure that the scene which I witnessed here is a re-enactment of identical mornings that have been seen on the beach at Poonthura over many centuries. During this time little will have changed. Today's nets, woven from synthetic fibres may be the only concession to modernity. The measured chanting and steady hauling of this morning's fishermen would have been familiar to their ancestors who knew equally well what it means to strain and suffer to make a living from the sea. These are men dignified by work, purposeful in their endeavours and proudly independent. Men deserving of admiration which I am sure comes there way far too infrequently. Theirs is a way of life built not upon choice but out of necessity. Their harvesting of the sea continues to provide the bedrock upon which many families in Poonthura have built their lives.

But for how much longer will this continue? Diminishing fish stocks and polluted oceans impact negatively upon the very existence of a way of life that has sustained and nourished the people of Poonthura for as long as history can recall. Now we may be approaching the end of time for a way of life that has provided the very identity of a whole community and a raison d'etre for generations of skilled men. It is to our shame that we bear witness to the erosion of the very fabric that has bound such communities together.

Hauling Nets

I hear chanting long before I see the men.
Along the shore their calls compete against the tide's percussive surge,
Bidding me come, draw nearer, calling come see, and then
Be one within the rhythm as man and nature here converge.
In efforts elemental passed through time,
This scene has been enacted for a thousand years,
Grandfather, father and so to son define
Routine, ritual and as the daily toil inheres,
More in hope than expectation hauling lines
That slowly drags the net against the tide,
Straining as fierce current and crushing waves confine,
Conspiring to confront and bruise your manly pride.
I stand in awe to see as spume and sweat unite
To challenge men to once more stand and fight.

The chanter's voice sounds out above the roar
of thrashing breakers bursting on the sand.
Urging all to strain their sinews to the haul
On ropes that chafe and blister every calloused hand.
Rhythm foretells labour and drives the efforts that they make.
Heels dig deep, shoulders tensed, arms like gnarled and polished
teak
Heave the line, just one more metre won with every new wave's
break
This and only this great effort will gain the victory they seek.
Purposeful and driven every man now owns his task
Knowing that each muscle strained will bring the harvest shore-
ward
With the bending of his back no man will ever think or dare to
ask
or yet to question how his salt stung life is ordered.
And now I see the silver shimmer 'neath the rippling of the foam
And hope the catch they make today will send these fine men
gladdened home.

Evening on the beach

Darkness demands greater care than earlier in the day as we
navigate the many obstacles, boats, makeshift storage huts and associated
detritus of the fishermen's labours. The sand is soft and warm as it
shifts and slides beneath our feet. Progress is slow, though Jament,
Johnson and Johnny, far more acquainted with this type of passage
than I, move with a confidence that serves only to emphasise my
awkwardness in unfamiliar surroundings. Beached boats loom from
the darkness, their shapes breaking the skyline like monuments in a
night-time memorial garden. They stand as a testament to the men who
put to sea and risk their lives in what to most, but perhaps not them, is

an alien environment. Subdued voices in the early night reveal small huddled groups of fishermen joined in conversation, quietly sharing thoughts as the day begins to close.

A place is chosen and we sit, forming our own small unkempt assembly. Settling on the ground I am sticky from the humidity and heat and soon my hands and feet are coated in the coarse sharp sand. At first we are silent as if gaining our bearings or awaiting some first conspiratorial words to bind us in common consent with regards to the direction for our discourse to proceed. In the near distance the ocean churns with waves roiling, breaking and lapping on the shore. This is a familiar noise, common to shorelines the world over, at once both reassuring and soothing in its constancy.

Jament, who rarely chooses to share his thoughts or seek the views of others, begins the conversation. He speaks slowly, the sing-song tones of Malayalam holding the attention of the group. Trying in vain to discern the gist of his speech I listen and await interpretation. "He wants to know", says Johnson, "if you have the same stars in England that we have here". So begins a conversation that lasts an hour or more whereby Jament tests me with questions about the world from which I have come. A world which in so many ways differs from his own, but which we soon find provides us with common issues and experiences to share.

Jament's words are carefully measured, almost spare. He speaks with a wisdom born of experiences which are beyond my intelligence, telling of things seen and done in the matter of fact manner usually reserved for the unexceptional. Johnson interprets Jament's words as he describes how, following the tsunami the fishermen encountered bodies floating on the sea. A terrible sight but one recounted in tones that suggest that life and death are never far away from the purview of men who put to sea in pursuit of fish. I ask him about the dangers and he acknowledges that these are ever present, though I gain an impression that they are faced with an acceptance born out of generations of lives committed to the sea.

Sharks, he says are not uncommon and can bring perils to the fishermen. He describes his own encounters with a shark that snatched a fish hooked on his line, thrashing angrily beneath the surface as it sensed the line and realised its own potential danger. "Caution is needed," he says. "Sharks are cunning, they will come to the surface and pretend that they are dead. They lie motionless lulling the fisherman into an ill-advised sense of security. They are never to be trusted". "What do you do in such a situation?" I ask, feeling naive the moment the words have left my mouth. "Each fisherman varies in his approach" I am told. "It is important to kill the shark, with an axe or by clubbing it, but whatever action you take, it is necessary to take care".

"Do you have fishermen in England?" Jament asks. A simple enough question but one that immediately has the effect of demonstrating the limitations of my knowledge. I try to explain how men from my own country over many centuries have gone to sea in search of fish, many species of which would be unknown in the warmer tropical oceans.

With such a limited knowledge I search for the words to describe how men trawl the deep, cold northern waters, facing icy storms and often savage winds. I try to paint a picture in words of oilskin clad fishermen on ships that venture away from the English coast, often embarking on missions of many days' duration in pursuit of cod. I explain how in the past the herring fishermen of Norfolk chased the 'silver darlings' through the North Sea bringing home a rich harvest, but how this trade has died as a result of declining numbers of fish. Jament listens and nods his head. This last description of dwindling fish stocks is one to which he can easily relate. I detect a sadness in his demeanour which prompts me to explain that my knowledge of the fishing industry in England is, to say the least limited and that I am giving him only a poor interpretation based upon a flimsy understanding. I suggest that perhaps when I return to England I could find for him a book with pictures of the fishermen of England. He likes this idea, nodding his assent.

Jament is an educated man. His is not the learning gained from books or formal schooling, but rather the wisdom gained from a lifetime of experiences. Here is a man who describes navigation by the stars, who knows all the indicators of the presence of shoals of fish and how to net or hook these to feed his family and a wider community. Jament reads the ocean as others read a book, he has retained mainly that knowledge that serves him every day. Those who may look from the outside at the fishermen of Poonthura may believe them to be ignorant of those aspects of learning that have come to be valued within the wider society. Such a view presents a narrow understanding of learning, one that fails to recognise the significance of an education that enables men to maintain the substance of communities.

The conversation wanes and as a group in unison we appear instinctively to know that it is time to go. One last look at the stars, so clear overhead tonight, assures me that I will remember this evening for being present when Jament shared one small part of his learning gained through generations of South Indian fisherman. I am in awe and have inadequate words to express my admiration for a man whose experiences and understanding represent a way of life which I can barely begin to comprehend.

Family Meals

Mealtimes signify a coming together of family and friends. This is true in most cultures and is certainly the case in India. In the evening, the business of the day concluded Jament and his family gather together on the veranda of his home. Rush mats are laid on the floor and the intensity of the aromas from the kitchen heighten the anticipation of the assembling family. Josie enters and urges us to sit and within moments the dishes begin to arrive. A steaming bowl of rice, a softer variety than that which is served in Karnataka is followed by a plate piled high with roti. And then the piping curries, kingfish and lentils in a delicate coconut gravy. As a guest I am urged to begin and require no second bidding. The fish served here is as good as I have experienced anywhere and the subtle flavours of the dishes served are an attestation to the culinary skills of the ladies of the household. The seated assembly feasts enthusiastically, savouring the spicy delicacies and eagerly replenishing plates with second helpings.

At the heart of proceedings Jament holds court. Surrounded by his family and friends he relaxes in their company. The conversation, invariably good natured, recalls events from the day and provides an opportunity to catch up with news as would be the case with any family at an evening meal. Together we probe our various experiences each asking questions to better understand our differing cultural experiences but finding more in common than of difference. Joe, Josie's husband and a relative newcomer to the family is clearly at ease with his new found companions as anyone would be where the hospitality is so warm.

The main course is done and a variety of fruits appear. Several kinds of banana, mango and jackfruit are served and all this followed by hot sweet tea. Little remains as our repast is complete. Contentedly we sit back and enjoy each other's company continuing our conversation and relishing memories of the day.

There is, of course nothing exceptional about such family mealtimes, except perhaps for this. Within this home I have been welcomed not only as a guest, but as an equal, made to feel valued for what I can offer in conversation and encouraged to share in the topics of the day. I find myself comfortably slipping into role as part of an extended family, privileged to share a private space with people who I have quickly come to regard as friends. In a few days' time I will be thousands of miles away in a different culture, living a different lifestyle that may be hard for Jament and some of his family to comprehend. I will return to my own family, pleased to be back with those I love and in the familiar environment of my own home. My time with Jament and with all of his family has enriched my life during these last few days and the memories of their companionship will continue to enhance my days for the future. For Jament as for myself, family is at the centre of life. To share in the life of a family is to be granted hospitality of the highest order.

One Fish, a Tapioca and a Bowlful of Rice

I realise this scene has been played out
Ten thousand times before.
The novelty is mine alone
Warmed by your hospitality
I seek to avoid embarrassing faux pas.

Mats spread out across the floor
You bid me sit and eat
Malayalam and English interwoven,
Though of the former I have none
I sit, watch and take my cue from others

This, a coming together of family,
Young and old sharing their repast
All new to me, so familiar to you
But you have welcomed me
I relax and see there are no strangers here

Only a simple open fire on which to make a banquet
What is the secret of such fine fare I ask?
One fish, a tapioca and a bowlful of Rice,
A coconut, some herbs and a handful of spice
With these simple items a family is satisfied.

(Not quite) lost in the lanes of Jayanagar

The English author Will Self, who until recently was a regular columnist in the *New Statesman*, has on a few occasions written about his predilection for exploring cities on foot. I recall, for instance, his vivid description of a nocturnal promenade with friends across London, and another account of him familiarising himself with the streets of Manchester. His assertion that if you really want to get to know a city the pedestrian option is most rewarding, is one to which I certainly subscribe.

Bangalore confuses me. Just as I grow in confidence that I recognise particular streets or districts, something happens that shatters this illusion. However, I am gradually familiarising myself with the area of Jayanagar where I have often stayed, and some form of orientation is gaining a tenuous foothold in my brain. Most mornings when staying here, before breakfast I explore the chaotic roads and potholed lanes a few strides away from my accommodation. These early morning perambulations have enabled me to form the beginnings of a mental map of this small quarter of Jayanagar. However, I still often find myself confused and lost amongst a maze of small houses, even smaller open fronted shops, assorted retail carts and a maelstrom of hurrying people making their way to somewhere from nowhere, or at least this is how it appears. At the same time, groups of lungi clad men slouch at street corners and despite an appearance of doing absolutely nothing, I suspect they are busily embarking upon business that I simply fail to recognise.

Each morning for the past week I have headed out in a different direction, and this morning, as has often been the case, I found myself lost in the back lanes somewhere beyond Madhevan Park. Buildings that appear familiar were not sufficiently embedded in my mind to be sure when last I was in their vicinity. Goods in shop windows that I convince myself I have viewed on earlier occasions, failed to provide me with sufficient detail to act as a point of reference. To put it simply, I was quite at a loss to be specific about my location.

I am aware that for many people, being lost is a state with which they are profoundly uncomfortable. Personally, I tend towards the view that as I am on foot, I cannot have ventured far from the familiar, and that a minor inconvenience such as not knowing where I am, increases my awareness and observation of the surroundings as I seek navigational clues. Like James Joyce's Leopold Bloom, I invariably encounter interesting people, and eventually end up on familiar ground. I am inclined to say that there is no such condition as being lost, but only an opportunity to explore new places.

This morning the labyrinthine lanes were as always, bustling with activity. A man, who looked as though he hardly had the strength to turn pedals, was calling out his wares as he sold fresh herbs from the back of a teetering, overloaded bicycle. As he weaved his way between dogs, resting cattle and women sweeping the thresholds of their homes, a woman dashed out from a doorway to stop him and purchase from his sweet smelling goods. Two men, greatly animated, negotiating noisily over a heap of coconuts, were in all probability far less angry than they sounded, though I never stayed long enough to see the outcome of their dispute. Two women chased a dog away from their property, uttering what I can only assume to have been Kannada oaths, then shared in a joke together, laughing and proffering to each other the typical South Indian head shake.

All the while, as I twisted and turned, negotiating my way between cow pats and potholes, giving a wide berth to a pair of mangy looking dogs, I enjoyed the sights and sounds of these unfamiliar streets and the nodded acknowledgement of friendly strangers. Bangalore is a city that seems never quite to be at rest. Its lanes and thoroughfares bustle with life from early morning until late at night. It must now be regarded as being in many ways as typical of metropolitan cities around the world, yet it retains in its back streets a certain charm that is perhaps reminiscent of an India that is fast disappearing.

Just as I was beginning to think that for once I really might be quite seriously lost, my reorientation was aided by chanting from the apparent near distance. Following the mesmeric sound I at last found its source and immediately recognised the temple from which it emanated. A few turnings later and I was standing beside the Kitturu Ranni Chennamma Stadium watching boys in a makeshift game of cricket, and knew that the rear of Madheven Park was only a few hundred metres away.

As I made my way back to my room for a shower and breakfast I found myself singing beneath my breath the famous words of John Newton – "I once was lost but now I'm found." This is only a temporary situation and I look forward to being not quite lost in a different set of lanes tomorrow morning.

Before the cacophony begins

6.00 am. It is still possible to enjoy a relatively quiet stroll around the back lanes of Jayanagar, but only with an early morning rise and by avoiding the already scuttling main thoroughfares. This is the coolest part of the day, though within ten minutes promenade I have already built up a sweat. It is also the time when it is possible to be more aware of the immediate surroundings of the city streets, as slightly less attention is needed to the tangled traffic than would be advisable later in the day.

Whether you are of any faith or none, it is impossible to ignore the religious influences on this, and any other Indian city. This morning alone, during the course of ninety minutes walking I must have passed twenty or more gaudily coloured temples, a church and two large mosques. These are features of the beating heart of the city, and I am mindful of the need to show respect to those worshippers who are offering their morning oblations to a range of deities. Fire, bells and water are an intrinsic feature of Hindu blessings, and located at a discreet vantage in order not to intrude, I watch as a white robed priest manipulates a fiery brass tray before his earnest supplicants. A black Ganesh, jasmine garlanded, takes in the proceedings from across the temple yard, whilst Hanuman gazes down from above, possibly offering support to the priest, or approval to the gathered assembly, or maybe both; I remain ignorant of the detail.

I note that often men and women stop in the road outside of the temples, and remove their sandals before offering Namaskara, with joined palms. This traditional greeting is said to be an acknowledgement of the divinity to be found in all human beings. After a short mumbled prayer, these devout petitioners slip back into footwear and return to their daily business. Others enter the sanctuary of the temple offering garlands or money in exchange for blessings to see them through another busy day.

A little way along the road I arrive in time to see the fevered activity of a dozen flower bearers as they prepare for today's wedding ceremony at the Kalyana Mantapa. Hoardings have been erected announcing the bride and groom and welcoming families to the sacred nuptials. Already a musician can be heard coaxing a rasping nadasvaram into tune. His labours along with those of his fellow band members will be long but joyful today.

Amidst the religious iconography and ceremonial preparations for the day, individuals are scurrying about their early morning labours. A lady belies her frail appearance as she pushes a barrow laden with fragrant herbs in the direction of central Jayanagar, another bears her burden of mangoes secure in a large round basket on her head. A flower seller, transporting his load on a rusting bicycle, its chain parched of oil, calls loudly to announce his presence to what he hopes will be eager buyers.

I am an obvious stranger on these streets, standing out from others and at times a feature of some curiosity. Children here, as elsewhere in the world are more bold and less reserved than most of the adult locals. They approach with beaming smiles and the more daring sometimes speak, often with a simple "how are you?" They delight in receiving a response and run giggling to their mates to report that they have accosted a foreigner and received a friendly reply.

Outside of a few houses elaborate rangoli patterns decorate the street, sadly within a short time they will be erased by passing feet, but at this time they are freshly made and welcoming in their intricacy. Lazy dogs sleep in odd corners, whilst others strut the streets and nose indelicately through litter and sacks of discarded detritus, in hope of half eaten fare. Some have adopted a strange air of superiority, seldom even glancing at the human elements of the ebb and flow of the streets while others presumably of lower status are ever guarded and watchful. Although they always appear harmless I am inclined to give them space as I pass by, thus probably justifying their assertion of ownership of the streets.

This area has a number of small parks and children's playgrounds. One I noted in particular this morning was well equipped with colourful slides, swings and roundabouts. My grandchildren would certainly have enjoyed these I thought. On a large open sports ground already I could count four games of cricket in action. I checked my watch which registered 7.10 - these boys are keen, no wonder Indian cricket is so strong. The players range from those entirely dressed in the traditional white attire, using top quality equipment, and bowling at a full set of stumps, to others with improvised wickets, and a patched up wooden implement that might once have looked more like an authentic cricket bat, but now resembles a worn and well taped cudgel.

By 7.30 the noise levels have already increased. As I approach Sri Aurobindo Marg the raucous blarting of horns and the rumble of buses and lorries increase in intensity. The calm of morning is fast disappearing to a familiar cacophony; relative slowness gives way to perpetual motion. My senses now are sharply focused on surviving the crossing of roads and avoiding the pavement potholes, as I return to my room to shower and breakfast. Tomorrow I will set off in a different direction and wonder at the human hotchpotch of the lanes of Jayanagar.

An Island Prison, or Respite from a High-rise Hell?

"How beautiful was the spectacle of nature not yet touched by
the often-perverse wisdom of man!"
Umberto Eco, *The Name of the Rose*

6.00 am. Even at this early hour the side roads radiating from Delhi's Aurobindo Marg are far from quiet as a small number of vehicles take advantage of a flow of traffic, easier to negotiate now than it will be in a couple of hours. This is probably the only time today when walking the roads and negotiating the onrushing traffic of Delhi feels relatively safe for pedestrians, forced to walk the kerbside by the multiple obstacles that have invaded the pavements. The few who I pass on my morning walk are well wrapped up against the November chill, and Johnson, my Keralite friend who accompanies me speaks of being cold. Having arrived here last night from a temperature of five degrees in England I am comfortable in lighter attire and know that there is every possibility that later today I will be feeling the heat.

As with most of my visits to India, my days will be fully occupied with teaching and meetings, which means that making opportunities during early mornings or late evenings is the only way in which I can educate myself about the immediate hinterland of the institutions where I work. My knowledge of Delhi is limited, but prior to this latest visit I had learned a little about the area called Sanjay Van in the location of Mehrauli, which I had deduced to be within a few minutes' walk from where I would be staying. Described as a "city forest" and the remnant of a formerly vast arboreal area along the Mehrauli South Central Ridge, this green area occupies almost 800 acres between Jawaharlal Nehru University and the historic Qutub Minar.

Lurid tales abound about the haunted nature of this quiet space, with some superstitious types who attach credibility to ghostly apparitions, suggesting that the spirit of the 14th-century Sufi saint Hazrat Sheikh Shahabuddin Ashiqallah, whose final resting place is located here, stalks the forest at night. More rational visitors to Sanjay Van come to experience a little tranquillity, or to enjoy the many birds, luscious trees and other natural phenomena which are plentiful here. Apparently more than 150 species of bird have been recorded and whilst walking the paths on our visit this morning in addition to the many peacocks I was aware of the raucous parakeets, dashing grey babblers and dancing myna birds, which were pleasant companions as we followed a path through a section of the wilderness. Overhead were wheeling black kites and at the Midway Lake a grebe was observed diving, presumably in search of a meal, and in the open spaces smart white egrets strode purposefully amongst the anthills.

Sanjay Van also provides shelter for an impressive number of recorded mammals and reptiles, and soon after starting this morning's walk we were greeted by a family of wild boar as they snouted through the low vegetation beside the path. Shortly after, a loping golden jackal viewed us with caution from amidst the scrubby bushes beneath our route, and a mongoose, having crossed before us peered from beneath a patch of greenery. More impressive still was a large Nilgai, or Blue Bull Antelope that held our interest for several minutes. It is an indication of how many visitors tread the paths of the forest, that this creature far from being alarmed by human presence, continued chewing the leaves from one of the lower branches of a peepal tree less than twenty feet from where we stood. I'm not sure if the same degree of indifference might be shown by any of the reputedly abundant snakes which dwell here, but I suspect that locals who display any of the symptoms of ophidiophobia may well give this place a wide berth.

Climbing a rocky path we gained a vantage point with the sun a fiery red ball just above the horizon to our right. Reaching the precipitous summit of the knoll the majestic figure of the Qutub Minar, as befits the world's tallest minaret, stood before us in the distance veiled in clouds, whilst beneath our feet mist whirled and rose between the kikar, rubber and drum stick trees. Such sights remain in the memory long after the day has passed, and I recognised the privilege that it was to be here in this moment.

Spaces such as this within the sprawling metropolis of Delhi afford a welcome respite from the din and frantic hustle that characterises much of the Indian capital. Though standing atop of the high ground and at Peacock Rocks in Sanjay Van this morning, enjoying the quiet, which was occasionally violated by yet another Dreamliner entering or leaving nearby Indira Gandhi airport, I wondered for how much longer this city besieged haven might survive. There must have been a time when green areas such as this were far more common in this region and when the creatures that have established their homes today in Sanjay Van were not imprisoned by the burgeoning concrete and tarmac that now restricts their territory. This is a place which is clearly treasured by many of the local people, including those who greeted us today as we met them along the broad sandy walkways and narrow paths, whilst negotiating a passage through a thorny landscape. I suspect however, that for the majority of Delhi's inhabitants Sanjay Van remains a mystery never to be visited and, in some cases, will remain completely unknown. This presents as something of a dilemma. If too many visitors arrive in this sensitive environment it might easily become degraded and the wildlife more disturbed. However, I am sure that if greater numbers were aware of the beauty of Sanjay Van, efforts for its conservation and demands to create more open spaces for public enjoyment might be demanded.

On being awarded the Schlich Memorial Forestry Medal in 1935, USA president Franklin D. Roosevelt stated that *"the forests are the lungs of our land, purifying the air and giving fresh strength to our people"*. Since then many others have referred to trees and forests as the lungs of the earth and have campaigned for their protection and in some instances have gone to prison, or even lost their lives in efforts to prevent their destruction. The contribution that trees make to our climate and to our health should not be underestimated, but the attention which is being given to the health of the trees themselves may sadly be too little and too late.

It trees truly are the lungs of the earth, I fear that in Sanjay Van there is evidence of severe pulmonary disease. Whilst this morning I could not actually hear the trees wheezing it seemed that this might simply be because they no longer have the strength to raise a cough. Running my fingers across what should have been a glossy emerald leaf, but was in fact dull and grey, I was hardly surprised to find that they came away covered in a film of particulates. For these lungs to continue in their service to humanity they need to photosynthesise, a process which depends upon the leaves absorbing sunlight; one which becomes increasingly difficult through a filter of dust.

The fact that today we met people in Sanjay Van who value this unique piece of Delhi for the contribution which it makes to both their physical and mental health, gives me some cause for optimism. It has been said that where there is life there is hope. If this is true, it may not be too late to revive what currently feels like an ailing wilderness body. Though it seems to me that time is short, the prognosis is not good and without immediate intervention this precious natural environment may be lost.

There was much of beauty and interest to be observed as we enjoyed our morning stroll through Sanjay Van and should I ever be in this part of Delhi in the future, I would not hesitate to return. I will long remember the relative tranquillity, the magnificent bird and mammal life, the rocky escarpments and rich vegetation, and I hope that future generations will have an opportunity to gain similar pleasure to that which I experienced today. As we made our way towards breakfast through the now heaving and fume belching traffic along a busy highway, gasping for the air, which makes up a small proportion of the gaseous concoction served up each day to the people of Delhi, I reflected on an hour and half well spent in the green sanctuary that is Sanjay Van.

I Shook the Hand of a Man Who Shook the Hand of Gandhi

It was during a visit to Trivandrum in 2011 that I happened to be passing the University of Kerala with friends and noticed a board indicating the Centre for Gandhian Studies. Having long had an interest in the life of the Mahatma and the history of the Indian struggle for independence, I persuaded my colleagues that we should make an impromptu visit, if only to find some information about the activities of this institution. Such curiosity often leads one along a blind alley and yields little by the way of new knowledge, occasionally however, the diversion made achieves unexpected results. This was most certainly the situation on this particular afternoon.

Entering the building into a rather nondescript vestibule there was a disappointing lack of evidence to suggest that this was anything other than a typical office reception area. I don't know what I had been expecting, but probably something more than a drab room with a few faded posters advertising long since passed events adorning the walls. My initial reaction was that there would be nothing here to command our attention and that this brief diversion from our afternoon walk would provide little of interest. However, just as we were about to turn and exit the building a young man appeared and politely enquired after the purpose of our visit. Explaining that we had seen the board announcing this as a Centre for Gandhian Studies, and that I had a particular interest in the achievements of the great man, I quickly appreciated that we had gained this young man's attention. Within minutes he had given us an explanation of the work of the centre, the nature of the courses and events organised and a breakdown of those academic staff who were involved in the management of the centre. Sadly he reported, this being a holiday period there was nobody other than himself available to enlighten us further.

Thanking our young informant for his time we made for the door but were halted when he enquired about our familiarity with the activism of K. E. Mammen, who he described as the Kerala Gandhi. I confess that at this point the name was unknown to me, but my Keralite friend Johnson was certainly familiar with the many protests and activities in which this ageing Gandhian had been involved. Asking for more information from the young custodian of the Gandhian Studies Centre, I found him both knowledgeable and effusive in his praise for the integrity of a man who had upheld principles of non-violence in his many campaigns for social justice throughout his life. As an added bonus he then offered to ring K. E. Mammen who lived close by and to see if he would be willing to meet with us, informing us that the great campaigner often welcomed visitors.

Mammen was born on 31 July 1921 in the Kerala city of Trivandrum (Thiruvananthapuram). He first came to prominence as an activist when he encouraged students to join the struggle for freedom from British rule at a public meeting held at Thirunakkara in Kottayam. Immediately seen as a potential threat to the authorities he was jailed for his activities, an act which far from dampening his spirits heightened his determination to stand up for equity and social justice. Following his imprisonment, the Diwan, Sir C.P. Ramaswami Aiyar ruled that no educational institution in Travancore should admit Mammen as a student, and he was indeed turned away by a number of establishments, including the Maharaja's College in Kochi. However in 1940 he was admitted to St Thomas' College, Thrissur, prior to joining the Madras Christian College. His return to studies was sadly short lived as two years later he was once again expelled for his continued participation in the Quit India campaign.

It was during the height of the Quit India movement that as a young man Mammen met and shook hands with Mahatma Gandhi during one of his visits to Kerala. This was a day which Mammen said he would never forget, and indeed it had a lasting effect on the rest of his life, which he endeavoured to live adhering as closely as possible to Gandhian principles.

Arriving at the door of K. E. Mammen's house we were greeted by a smiling lady who welcomed us and suggested that we might enjoy a cup of tea and refreshments during our visit, before ushering us into a small, well-furnished room where the Kerala Gandhian rose from an armchair to greet us. The warmth of his smile and the firmness of his handshake immediately put us at ease, and as he beckoned us towards comfortable chairs it was apparent that the young man at the university had been correct in his assertion that K. E. Mammen enjoyed company and welcomed visitors.

The next hour passed quickly as we drank tea and listened attentively as our host told us of his experiences as an activist and advocate for the rights of marginalised individuals and groups. More recently his stand against the sale of alcohol had made significant demands on his time, though during our brief meeting he made us aware of the number of iniquities, which he believed needed to be confronted not only in Kerala but across the wider world. In particular he reminded us of our responsibilities to speak out against injustice and to represent those whose voices struggle to be heard. He left us in no doubt that his advancing years had done little to diminish either his passion or his ability to keep abreast of current affairs. The room in which we were seated was furnished with many artefacts from his eventful life, including several Christian images, many from the Syrian Orthodox church, with which had enjoyed a far from compliant relationship over a number of years. But amongst his most prized memorabilia were those associated with the freedom struggle including articles associated with those times and letters written by Gandhiji.

It is rare that on so brief an acquaintance one comes away from a meeting feeling that time had been spent with an individual deserving of the utmost accolades and respect. On walking away from K.E. Mammen's home that day I felt honoured to have shared these moments with him. The great Gandhian died on July 26th 2017 at the age of 96 and was cremated at Santhi Kavadam in Trivandrum with full state honours at a ceremony attended by a cardinal, a bishop and Minister Kadannappally Ramachandran. As a man who whilst respectful of individuals of such high office, regarded them as no more important than those disadvantaged members of the community on behalf of whom he waged several of his campaigns, I feel sure he would have been especially delighted had he been able to see the many hundreds of activists and supporters from both the local community and further afield who gathered to honour this great freedom fighter.

Many of the obituaries written in K.E. Mammen's honour were effusive in their praise for a man of integrity and determination. Several such accolades appeared in newspapers, which on numerous occasions had found themselves in opposition to his campaigns. Such is the nature of activism which invariably raises hackles but also attracts a certain element of begrudging respect. I personally feel grateful and honoured that I had an opportunity to shake the hand of a man who shook the hand of Gandhi.

Death of an Ambassador

In common with probably tens of thousands of other visitors to India, my first encounter with the chaos of Indian traffic was made from the back seat of an Ambassador. These icons of the Indian roads, the first cars made in India and modelled on the British Morris Oxford, rolled off the production line from 1957 until an announcement in 2014 signalled its demise bringing to a halt production of this unique car by the Hindustan Motor Company.

For many years the Ambassador was the vehicle of choice for leading Indian politicians and diplomats, eager to demonstrate their loyalty to national industry, and these rumbling masters of the tarmac (those small areas of the road that can occasionally be found between potholes!) were often fitted with "luxury" items such as interior fans and curtains. Sadly those days have gone and it was noticeable that in recent election campaigns the leaders of all political parties, including the Prime Minister Narendra Modi, chose to parade around the country in flash air conditioned SUVs.

I remember with great affection the arrival of myself and Sara in India in the summer of 2000. Leaving the airport to be slapped around the face by a blast of heat, we were affectionately greeted by the highly efficient Sudha from the Krishnamurti Foundation, who was to steer us through our first uncertain days in Chennai. Following her across the airport carpark, through a maze of sleeping bodies, roguish looking dogs and vendors squatting on their haunches selling a range of wares, we eventually met a driver, who having deposited our luggage in the boot urged us into the rear seat of his car. From the front bench seat Sudha assured us that at this early hour of the morning the traffic would be light, and we would soon reach our destination in Greenways Road.

With a slight judder and a cloud of black acrid fumes we were soon under way and making ponderous progress into the streets of Chennai, driven by our bare footed chauffeur who appeared at times to be wrestling with an uncooperative oversized steering wheel. Meandering around a hundred obstacles, including cattle, goats and tight muscled, sinuous men pushing handcarts, surely loaded way beyond their safe capacity, we settled back on the leather seat for what we were soon to learn was a typical Indian city journey. Skilfully our driver eased the vehicle through gaps that appeared to miraculously part before him, as with great nonchalance he negotiated the route into Chennai city. Before long we came to realise that in India when they build a car they must follow a particular order. The importance of the horn is such that I am convinced that this is the very first component to be made, around which all others are gradually constructed. The continuous cacophony of blarting horns is a sound for ever associated with the roads of India and to this day provides a grating, discordant symphony that is the background to urban Indian life.

During that first journey our curiosity was immediately aroused and questions to Sudha caused her some amusement. "On what side of the road is the driver supposed to drive?" we enquired. "Well, really on the left, but basically this is not always possible, so wherever there is a space." "How many lanes are there on this road?" not too unreasonable a question I thought. "Well officially two, but the road is plenty wide enough for more," we were informed as the traffic inched forward, vehicles often six or more abreast, through the heaving procession of cars, colourful painted lorries, smoke belching buses, auto-rickshaws, handcarts, wagons pulled by cattle, cycles and motorcycles, often bearing entire families . "Are the roads always this busy?" "This is the quiet part of the day, later the traffic will increase greatly." So continued our incredulous conversation until we reached the quiet haven of Vasanta Vihar, our destination amongst the relative tranquillity of trees and lawns in the heart of Chennai city.

Gradually after the initial shock and a few days of finding our way around the streets in an auto-rickshaw we became inured to the chaos of Indian roads and now, twenty years later, when incidentally the traffic is far worse than on that first visit, I have become in common with most of the locals, a genuine fatalist, taking to the roads in cars and auto rickshaws with the naïve nonchalance of a traveller who has become complacent in the face of ever impending danger. Though I cannot say that I am ever totally relaxed!

Of course it will not be everyone who mourns the demise of that doyen of the Indian roads the humble Ambassador. In July 2014 the journalist Hormazd Sorabje writing about the passing of the Ambassador on the BBC website claimed that: "You needed really strong triceps to work the ridiculously heavy steering, the deftness of a surgeon to slot home the spindly column shifter into each gear (shifting from second to third gear was an art form) and immense strength to make the car stop - you had to nearly stand on the brakes". I suspect that in celebrating the end of one era of motoring that even Mr Sorabje could not have anticipated the chaos that has resulted from the expansion of the new breed of cars that today strangle the final vestiges of life from Bangalore's city streets.

These days, when climbing aboard a taxi in India it is more likely to be of modern European, Korean or Japanese manufacture, fitted with the latest sound system, air-conditioning, power steering, seat belts and a reliable set of brakes. Ambassadors are still seen, and it is noticeable that in some instances these are treasured by their owners, immaculately maintained and driven with pride. An ever dwindling number of Ambassador taxis are in operation, I have used them over the past couple of years from Trivandrum airport and in Panaji, and they remain a constant presence in Kolkata, but it seems that most taxi drivers and probably their passengers too, aspire to something more plush and modern.

A few years ago in New Delhi with my good Indian friends, Jayashree, Johnson and Lisba we were faced with a considerable choice of vehicles on the taxi stands in the city. Perhaps it was just nostalgia that enabled me to persuade my patient colleagues that a rotund and shiny, black and yellow Ambassador was a better choice than one of the slick modern cars that also occupied the row of awaiting cabs. The choice as it happened was a good one, for this car was piloted by an excellent Sikh driver who clearly new the streets of Delhi well. We took his cell phone number and kept him busy for much of the week. Bouncing around the worn springs of the bench seats we experienced a ride similar to that which I imagine many of India's great names from the past, Jawahrala Nehru, Indira Gandhi and Rajiv Gandhi amongst them must have endured over many years in order to demonstrate their patriotic commitment. Today, whenever I see one of these magnificent machines on the streets of of an Indian metropolitan city, I am almost tempted to salute. I am glad to have had this opportunity to experience a genuine piece of Indian history, and even now I hope that the affection that many have for this most recognisable symbol of the roads of India may enable it to be saved from oblivion. However, I fear that the continued rush towards modernisation may mean that in a few years we will be mourning the death of the Ambassador.

Hanging on to the Past: Rickshaw Town, Kolkata

When I wrote the previous article in this collection, titled "Death of an Ambassador." This had nothing whatsoever to do with international diplomacy, but rather presented a personal reflection on the gradual disappearance of the once common motor vehicle, that was so much a feature of the highway landscape of India. A decision to cease manufacture of a car which was favoured by so many Indians, from government ministers to taxi drivers, was probably a result of the demands made by drivers for the latest models of motor vehicle, which today choke the roads and lanes of every metropolitan city. When visiting Bangalore, Chennai, Trivandrum or other cities in the south of India in recent years I have still seen the occasional rounded features of an Ambassador making its ebullient path through the tidal mass of traffic. As previously stated, at such times I find myself reminiscing about my first ventures on to the roads of Chennai in 2000, seated with my wife on the leather upholstered rear seat of one of these magnificent beasts.

It is not possible to hold back the ravages of time and in this regard we all need to come to terms with change. I have long been reconciled to the fact, that as time passes it has become less likely that I will have an opportunity to once more travel in style in one of these stately chariots. It was therefore a matter of considerable surprise and not a little pleasure, that on arriving for the first time in the city of Kolkata I noted that the majority of the taxis filling the serried ranks at the airport gate comprised bright canary yellow Ambassadors. Whilst I was grateful that arrangements had been made to meet me at the airport to ferry me into the city, I must admit to a slight disappointment that I was to be conveyed in a shiny modern Korean manufactured vehicle, rather than in one of these old friends. I have noted that as I get older nostalgia plays an increasing role in my life. Perhaps I need to be more tolerant of the disappearance of those formerly familiar elements of the past and learn to embrace the "progress" that I see all around me.

On the basis of a very short stay in Kolkata, I am inclined to suggest that for those who seek a glimpse into India from an earlier period, this may well be a rewarding city to visit. In the architecture, some of which maintains a tentative toe hold to an imperial past, (thankfully now banished to the history books), there is much to be admired and celebrated. Time for tourism is rare during my frequent visits to this country, but an all too brief visit to the magnificent Victoria Monument provided more than enough evidence of the might that was asserted by British colonial power, which once imposed itself upon this country and its people with Kolkata (Calcutta) as its centre of administration. This building and others nearby, including the resplendent General Post Office are both a tribute to the more creative elements of the British occupation, and an indication of the messages of control, which were to be conveyed to the local inhabitants of the city. Such splendour enhances this former Indian capital, but must have been regarded with mixed emotions during Victoria's long reign.

To friends in India I have often bemoaned the fact that elegant buildings from earlier generations have been allowed to erode and degrade in Indian cities. A prime example of this is the once elegant school attended by the great educator, philosopher and statesman Sarvepalli Radhakrishnan in Chennai. I was greatly saddened when I visited the site of this once fine seat of learning to find it in a state of disrepair and abused by the dumping of piles of rubbish around its premises. I know that many fine buildings must have been lost to the city of Kolkata, but others have been beautifully conserved and form a fine backdrop to the city's daily life.

A further link to an earlier age in Kolkata is fostered by the continuing presence of cycle rickshaws, which remain as a favoured mode of transport for many citizens of this sprawling city. I have seen a few of these man-powered conveyances in other parts of India, notably near the Chepauk cricket stadium in Chennai, but here in Kolkata they are a common sight and in constant demand by local people requiring transport for short journeys. I watched yesterday evening with great admiration, as a spindly rickshaw pilot laboured against his pedals to transport two large ladies and their well laden shopping bags to their chosen destination. The stature of the rickshaw driver is seldom a fair indicator of his strength, as demonstrated by this wiry hard working man. Many of the rickshaws are brightly decorated; some with religious iconography, pictures of Bollywood heroes, or colourful floral paintings and several are adorned with additional tinsel, flowers and ribbons. Their owners exhibit pride in their machines and I am sure that those with the most colourful displays have an advantage when seeking a fare.

This morning I walked through lanes less than a mile from where I am staying in a small hotel in the Kasba district of Kolkata, which I have already come to think of as Rickshaw town. At 6.30 in these narrow lanes amidst ramshackle huts made of the detritus of the city, people were engaged in their morning ablutions. Water ran freely from hosepipes utilised by the local inhabitants who showered, cleaned their teeth and managed their laundry in preparation for the working day. These local occupants of this crumbing suburb are poor, though the banter in which they engaged as I wove my way between multiple obstacles and sleeping dogs on the street, indicates a positive community spirit. Alongside almost every small dwelling fringing these lanes, cycle rickshaws were parked and piled all around were spare wheels, tyres, chains, pedals and other components essential to keep these vehicles on the road. Mangy dogs and squawking fowl scurried around the scene or lazed around in the dust, whilst children chased in and out of each other's houses. This is an area founded upon the pride and hard labour of the cycle rickshaw men, who will later in the day compete for fares in order to feed, clothe and provide the most basic essentials for the survival of their families. If work truly is worship, then these hard working men live their lives as supplicants to a hard deity. They do so with great dignity and pride in their labour.

While central Kolkata displays much of the grandeur of its imperial past, in these lanes I witnessed scenes, which I suspect have changed little since the period when those magnificent buildings which enhance the city were erected. Today many statements are made by politicians and businessmen who would have us believe that the Indian economy is healthy and indeed burgeoning. It is certainly evident that the numbers of the middle class Indian population who have disposable income have increased. In Kolkata as in other Indian cities the skyline is fast changing as high-rise buildings and the snaking route of the metro emerge as dominant features of the urban landscape. International retail outlets, identical to those found on any European city street advertise their fashionable wares beneath neon signage, and the ubiquitous pizza and burger parlours abound. Financial benefits and security have been brought to many as a result of modernisation and enterprise, though it seems that the vagaries of the Indian stock market are having little impact upon the poorer members of Indian society who inhabit those rude dwellings which characterise Rickshaw town. Here as elsewhere in the world, the gap between the haves and the have-nots is widening and not all are benefitting from a strengthening economy.

As I walked the lanes of this area I reflected on the writings of a great Bengali, the Nobel Laureate economist Amartya Sen who must have often walked the very streets that I had been exploring over recent days. He has quite rightly emphasised that *"poverty is not just a lack of money; it is not having the capability to realize one's full potential as a human being."* In observing the rickshaw men preparing for another tough day on the lanes of Kolkata, I could not help but think that the determination to meet the needs of their families displayed by these fine individuals, is an indication of exactly the untapped potential that Sen had in mind.

The cycle rickshaw makes a nostalgic conjunction between modern India and its past. In twenty years I suspect that the only rickshaws that will remain will be utilised as a means of supporting Kolkata's tourist trade. Just as the once famous trams of Kolkata have become limited to a few lines which ensure the security of the city's heritage trail, so are the cycle rickshaws and the Ambassador taxis likely to fall victim to the same fate. But what then will be the future of those individuals who ply their trade turning the pedals of those most environmentally sound cycle rickshaws, and how will they then maintain their lives in the community that is today, rickshaw town? These are questions which I hope are at the forefront of deliberations amongst politicians and policy makers in India. If this is not the case then someone needs to remind them of their responsibilities to all Indians, not only those who have prospered from urbanisation and the Indo-technological revolution.

If I really must go shopping, there is only one place to head for!

I dislike shopping. That is, I am intolerant of the endless mind-numbing browsing of groaning shelves and sagging racks of items that I can live quite happily without and which can succeed in holding my interest for no more than a few seconds. Friends and family are acutely aware of my aversion to a pastime that apparently some claim to find therapeutic, (if this kind of therapy is really needed, I suggest that more drastic psychiatric interventions might prove beneficial!), and have accepted defeat in their efforts to drag me through the doors of various department stores or other retail outlets.

I fully accept that my attitude to pastimes of the retail variety may be perverse, and like many who exhibit such finely defined phobias, I am happy to confess that there is one great exception to this personal odium. Whilst it takes considerable efforts by wild horses to drag me kicking and screaming into the average supermarket or bon marché, I am always delighted to pass an hour or two in a good bookshop. Let me be clear, I am not writing here about those multi-cloned bookshop chains that are to be found on every town or city high street, though I recognise that these often provide the only option for the local reading population and I have on occasion found the staff within these largely characterless institutions to be well-informed and helpful. My concern is far more focused on the independent booksellers, many of whom stock treasures that are seldom to be discovered on the shelves of the multi-national stores. Sadly in this digital age of on-line purchasing, these great servants of the high street have become an endangered species, though a few determined independent booksellers do continue to offer a first class service to the discerning bibliophile. Such defenders of the faith take pride in feeding the habits of the avid book collector and reader, ensuring that their greatly respected wares are sold only to those most likely to afford them the comfort of a well-ordered bookshelf in a good home. Long may they thrive!

In England as elsewhere, the ease of ordering books on-line, which are then delivered with great efficiency to the reader's front door, has sadly become the main assassin of a good number of independent bookshops. I can fully appreciate why this has happened, and when one compares the prices at which books are available from the larger on-line stores with those of most bookshops, it is easy to see how they have come to dominate. But I would still make a case for the need for good independent bookshops run by knowledgeable booksellers, who have a passion for the printed word and a desire to interact at a personal level with their customers.

Near to where I live, whilst a significant number of well-loved bookshops have disappeared in recent years – I still miss Paddy Fox and her welcoming smile in the bookshop in Brixworth; a few remain and whilst clinging on with their finger nails, continue to offer an excellent service. Quinn's in Market Harborough, Old Hall Bookshop in Brackley and the Courthouse bookshop in Oundle are survivors who have thus far escaped the executioner's axe to which so many others have fallen victim. Though I suspect that their owners are for ever looking over their shoulder's lest the grim reaper should appear.

The on-line retail phenomenon has not only struck at bookshops in the UK, but has had a similar effect in much of the world, including India. In the many years that I have been visiting Bangalore I have seen a number of first rate book sellers disappear, and they are greatly missed. I recall the excellent service provided by Strand Book Shop whose highly efficient proprietors in 2000 shipped a dozen books for me from Bangalore to England. They arrived three months after being ordered, beautifully wrapped and stitched in sail cloth, and having been read are now safely nestled alongside others on the shelves in my study, regularly taken down for reference, or simply to strengthen and renew acquaintance. I was greatly saddened a few years ago when seeking out this professionally managed emporium to find it replaced by an outlet selling... well I've no idea what it was selling, why would I have ever bothered to have entered the doors?

Higginbotham's continues to house a fine array of titles and Gangaram's Book Bureau in Sivanchetti Gardens just off Mahatma Gandhi Road maintains a good selection, though it lacks the personality that would make it a more welcoming establishment to the dedicated reader. However, one wonderful store attracts me like iron filings to a magnet whenever I am in Bangalore and is the epitome of what I regard as the perfect bookshop. Nagasri Book House hidden away in the corner of a bustling indoor market near the bus station in Jayanagar 4th Block, is a haven in which several hours can be constructively passed. Here one can find dedicated guardians of the merest opuscule and the greatest magnum opus, each treated with respect and handled with due reverence.

Nagasri, run by two knowledgeable and enthusiastic gentlemen who are delighted to discuss books, authors and publishers for as long as you have time available, can be no more than twelve feet deep and ten wide, yet it is a veritable cornucopia of riches. Books are stacked from floor to a fifteen-foot ceiling, with two narrow passages between, in which at most half a dozen customers can safely graze at any one time. There is a haphazard order to the place (if you think that to be a contradiction of terms, you are probably not a devoted bookshop browser), which once you crack the code, reveals treasures unbounded. Within each towering stack can be found well esteemed classics, shoulder to shoulder with obscure scholarly disquisitions, long established authoritative treatises and brief trifles of local trivia, each comfortable between its own covers and alongside total strangers. Within this Aladdin's cave, fingering through columns of rainbow coloured spines is to explore new worlds and old in anticipation of reminders of the past and unexpected discoveries. Furthermore, if fatigued after a day's work you are unable to locate exactly what is sought, I can guarantee that the expert Mr Prasad, proprietor of this nirvana will put his hands almost instantly upon the volume required.

Having visited this site of pilgrimage at least three times a year for the past few years I know that on each arrival Mr Prasad will have already identified a number of titles which he believes may be of interest. Like all good book lovers he makes suggestions and offers critical comments, but never has he attempted to sell to me something which would not hold my interest, and he never complains when I reject his wares having already acquired copies elsewhere, or simply because other books are of more interest. His strategy is a sensible one as I estimate that at least a hundred of the several thousand books on my shelves at home originated from Nagasri.

My study at home possesses many tomes discovered and taken back to England from the Nagasri treasure house, which I am sure I would never have found in my local Northamptonshire bookshops, including several by local Bangalore resident writers such as the historian Ramachandra Guha, (himself a customer of Nagasri) along with works of Indian history, poetry, art, philosophy and literature with which I was previously unfamiliar, and which few local bookshops in England would find it in their interest to stock. The shop – nay, this is far too trivial a term – this oasis amidst the desert wastes of Bangalore, has become an abode of peace and safety amongst the non-stop blur of motion that is Jayanagar. I am therefore not surprised when I find that it is held in the affection of book loving Bangalorian acquaintances who praise both its stock and the service of its excellent proprietors.

Long may the independent bookshop flourish, with its distinctive smells and textures, its well laden shelves and its sage custodians of knowledge. Thank you to all who buck the trend and refuse to buckle beneath the digital age, which threatens to eradicate the sensuous pleasures of book browsing. And a particular cheer for Nagasri Book House and its dedicated managers.

See you on my next visit.

J.S. Khanderao: Through the Window

The artists whose work I most admire are those who provide evidence of having continually sought new means of expression throughout their lives. The genius who comes most readily

to mind in this respect has to be Picasso. The great Spanish artist is often referred to in relation to the different periods of his career during which it was possible to discern a distinctive change in his style and the manner in which he looked at the world. Examples of this can be seen in his Blue Period from the early years of the twentieth century, which gave way to the Rose Period and later still his experiments with cubism, which differed greatly from the Neoclassicism and surrealism to be found in his work between the two world wars and his eventual experiments with a form of neo-expressionism. Throughout his life Picasso refused to be categorised or restricted in his work by the demands of the art establishment. Always a leader and never a follower, he kept the art world guessing by drawing upon a vast range of influences and personal interests, such as African masks and performers from circus and stage, and experimented with a wide range of media and techniques. At the city museum and art gallery in Leicester, a city not too far from where I live, there is a magnificent collection of Picasso's work in ceramics, which when viewed leaves one in no doubt about his versatility and genius. Critics bothered him not at all because of the confidence which he rightly had in respect of his ability to innovate and challenge the conventions of the day. His was truly a restless mind fired by a great imagination and boundless energy and this I suspect was what enabled him to create works that will certainly endure.

In the UK we have been blessed with a number of great artists who, whilst perhaps not gaining the notoriety and acclaim attached to Picasso have none the less demonstrated a great ability to reassert themselves throughout their lives, by changing direction and creating works that cause those critics who have become comfortable with their oeuvre to raise an eyebrow. David Hockney and John Piper are two such artists who through their works demonstrated the courage to move beyond the techniques with which they had become associated early in their careers, to challenge themselves through experimentation and adventures into new forms of creativity. These and other artists of their ilk, Paul Cezanne and Freda Kahlo come immediately to mind, are able to combine the most astute observation of the world with the sharpness of imagination, which enables us to see everyday images in a manner that has previously eluded our attention. Whilst the work of some artists is instantly recognisable as being of the creator's well defined and undoubtedly brilliant established style, I find the work of those who are for ever seeking new creative pastures infinitely more interesting.

It was undoubtedly my fascination for artists who have an unsettled and possibly unsettling way of depicting the world that contributed to the great pleasure, which I gained from a retrospective exhibition of the works of the Kannadiga painter Jagadevappa Shankarappa Khanderao presented at the National Gallery of Modern Art in Bangalore. Housed in the beautiful Manikyavelu Mansion, the gallery space is not the easiest to manage. With numerous small rooms housing an eclectic collection of works and a few larger spaces, which were fully utilised for this retrospective exhibition titled *"Through the Window,"* I can well imagine that the curators had a difficult task in arranging the hanging of the significant corpus of work on display. Indeed the fact that they managed to achieve a level of cohesion that enabled the visitor to follow a logical developmental path through the life of the artist is something for which they deserve the highest praise.

In the early stages of the exhibition, a series of still life paintings depicting the traditional subjects of the artists craft; fruit, bottles and a range of textures that enable the painter to show off his undoubted skills, were similar to those created by artists exhibited in many of the galleries of Europe. In this sense they were unexceptional. Some of the works of Paul Gaugin from the latter years of the nineteenth century came immediately to mind when viewing these particular pictures. But then by way of a contrast a series of water colour pictures created *en plein air* in locations including Hampi and Surpur present with a delicacy of touch and capture natural light and shadow, not unlike the work of the English water colourist John Sell Cotman in his depiction of buildings such as Caister Castle in Norfolk. Water colour painting is often mistakenly seen as the domain of the gifted amateur, but in the pictures created by Khanderao in this exhibition one can easily see the immensity of this man's talent. These pictures stand comfortably shoulder to shoulder with the finest exponents of the water colour media from Europe with which I am more familiar, and viewing them here in Bangalore I was reminded of an exhibition I once attended that included the works of John Crome and Henry Bright; artists who caused me to reappraise my earlier belief that working in this media was in some way less demanding than that deployed by the artist who paints in oils.

However, oils have also proven to be a forte of this fine Indian painter. Landscape is clearly important to Khanderao, but here is an artist who is not content to rest on his laurels, a man who having demonstrated his abilities with watercolour extends his explorations through the application of oils. Whilst many of his works present us with a true representation of a place set in a particular time, there are occasions when his landscape begins to veer towards the abstract, as for example in the canvas titled *"Creative Landscape"* painted in 1982. Perhaps here we have a precursor of the most recent of Khanderao's work presented at this exhibition, of which I will say more later, which makes use of bold shapes and muted colours to draw the viewer into a space where perspective is cleverly enhanced by the positioning of two simply drawn birds.

As with Picasso, Khanderao appreciates the importance of having a good understanding of line and space to create his works. In a manner similar to the great Spaniard he demonstrates this level of awareness through a series of pencil drawings in which he captures both the character and subtle movement of the many local individuals who populate his sketches. One particular drawing from 1969 of a woman squatting on her haunches, an expression of alertness captured in her face and the folds of her saree falling naturally about her form, demonstrates empathy and an astute understanding of the artist's subject, which is so seldom captured in the images produced by lesser artists. Others in which the he is clearly observing the varying tensions and balance of a young man in a series of drawings from 1967 provide unique insights into the ways in which Khanderao is honing the skills that enabled him to become such a significant creator of figurative art.

A series of pictures depicting the folk traditions including Bhuteru and Puravantaru from Khanderao's native North Karnataka painted in the early years of the twenty first century has certainly benefitted from the commitment, which the artist devoted to studying movement, shape and form in the earlier drawings. Here once again the use of light and shadow to capture the movement of performers creates illusions of depth and intensity of emotion as Khanderao experiments with earthy colours such as those with which I am more familiar in some of the works of Paul Klee. Circus performers, acrobats and other itinerant street artists have provided a rich source of inspiration to many artists. Such characters were inevitably captured in the works of Picasso, though even he takes second place to the Irish painter Jack Yeats in this particular subject area. Khanderao must certainly have a good understanding of the lives and rituals in which his subjects engage in order to have produced these vibrant images.

As a visitor who was until this day totally unfamiliar with Khanderao's work, the greatest surprise which I experienced was with his most recent work. Here in this exhibition were contrasting images, which were it not for the information provided I would have taken to be the works of two different artists. Firstly a series of classically styled and formal portraits, including one of S.M. Pandit painted in oils in 2015 hark back to a period of John Lavery or Georgina Agnes Brackenbury and their contemporaries. But then, from the same decade a series of abstract pictures which deal playfully with the light falling through windows could not be much further distanced in terms of style and form. Here again some connection to the use of shapes and space in the work of the Swiss artist Paul Klee came to mind, though in Khanderao's window series there is as much emphasis upon light as there is on shape.

An hour and a half spent at this exhibition was time well invested and my only disappointment is that I had no time to return at a later date before the conclusion of the show. My ignorance of Khanderao's work has to some extent been addressed, though I would need far more hours to fully appreciate the genius that is so evident in his art. This retrospective provided a fitting tribute to a man whose work demonstrates diversity, a nuanced view of the world and a commitment to continually develop and polish his skills. I may not have known his work prior to this visit, but I will certainly look out for it in the future.

Long Live the cows of Jayanagar!

Over the years of visiting India I have become rather fond of cows. These amiable, docile creatures are probably the least offensive of road users in the country, and are most certainly deserving of the respect that they generally receive from the Bangalorians. I often stop to pass the time with one or two of these bovine wanderers when out on my early morning promenade of the local streets. Though I confess the conversation tends to be limited, as I suspect that the average Bangalore cow has a limited appreciation of English and my Cow-Kannada is all but non-existent.

I suppose that in common with most English visitors to India, when I first visited the country I was somewhat taken aback to find so many cows occupying the streets of a major metropolis. But now I find that they are one of the more soothing features of the urban landscape, quieter than the average street occupant, and a welcome sight as they amble along the roads and lanes of Bangalore. Furthermore I have come to realise that they perform a number of essential functions without which the city would be a poorer place.

The most obvious contribution made by these citizens of the streets is that of providing milk. Indeed this morning whilst meandering through the back lanes beyond Madhavan Park, I paused for a while to watch a lady milking a most tranquil black and white animal as it chewed methodically through a pail of vegetation that she had provided. The usual grazing available to the local cows in the city is unusual to say the least, and I wonder about the quality of the milk obtained.

A second function and one that is most obvious to anyone who explores these streets, is the hopeless attempt that the cows make to manage the rubbish that lays on almost every street corner. There are times during the year, such as the Dussehra festival, that must be greatly welcomed by these would be refuse managers, as the litter over which they pick is greatly enhanced by fruit and coconuts used and then discarded in many ceremonies. I have noted near the rooms where I stay, a particular pile of rubbish which is greatly favoured by several black cows who have been regular visitors, exploring the menu and then eating their fill. The local crows are clearly disturbed by this behaviour and have certainly been pushed some way down the pecking order as they hover and bounce around awaiting their turn to dine. Even the beady eyed black kites appear respectful of the cows, often circling above but seldom disturbing their pasture.

A major contribution that these beautiful creatures make to the city is one that I suspect is overlooked by many, but may be a source of frustration to a few. I have noted that they are the most efficient traffic calmers. A few days ago I witnessed two guerrilla tactics adopted by cows in order to assert their authority on the streets. In the first instance a very large and confident black cow simply lay down in the street forcing every vehicle to slow down and weave a cautious passage around the reclining beast. Several drivers hooted, but the cow was unimpressed having found a wholly suitable space for an afternoon rest and being determined to assert her rights. Incidentally, although this cow herself had two fine horns, she never saw the necessity to honk back! Later that same day I noticed two cows, one black and white, the other brown working most efficiently in tandem. Strolling methodically and at a leisurely pace along the centre of a main road, they had developed the technique of rhythmically rocking from side to side and avoiding travelling in anything that might resemble a straight line. The effect was dramatic. Much of the traffic was hesitant to pass and the bustle of the city street was albeit temporarily, calmed.

So it is you see that I have come to admire and appreciate the many virtues of these wonderful animals. They are truly the matriarchs of the road and play so many essential roles in maintaining the equilibrium of Bangalore. Such are their qualities that I think on my return home I may send a recommendation to the council in Northampton, suggesting that a herd or two of cattle might be an excellent addition to the town centre!

Long Live– the cows of Jayanagar!

Looking Beyond the Boundaries

A few years ago, I received a thoughtful email from a lady, a former journalist who I had never met, sent from her home in Karachi. My correspondent was the grandmother of one of my students who was about to graduate having completed studies for her PhD. The message expressed regret that because of her age and various infirmities she would be unable to attend her granddaughter's graduation and she thanked me for the support and tuition that I had provided during her years of study in England. In all honesty her granddaughter had been an excellent student and the task of guiding her through her research and writing had not been onerous. However, the kind words expressed in the mail were greatly appreciated and I responded to thank the lady for her affirmation of my work.

When next I met my student, which if my memory serves me well was a couple of days before her graduation, I shared her grandmother's mail and expressed my gratitude for her kind words. During the course of our conversation it was revealed that my correspondent was now in her eighties and whilst mentally alert found long journeys physically uncomfortable, hence her regrets at not being able to travel to witness the pomp and ceremony of an English university graduation. Happily, her daughter, my student's mother, was to be present at this event and would doubtless have shared joyful memories and photographs on her return to Pakistan. It was during the course of our conversation that I commented to my student, that when her grandmother had been born, more than ten years before 1947, she would of course have been an Indian. Whilst this fact was not new to my student, I suspect that for a young woman who had never known a time before the existence of Pakistan, it was not a matter that had warranted a great deal of thought.

Whilst it would be unfair to say that the line drawn by Sir Cyril Radcliffe, which bifurcated the states of Punjab and Bengal in his role as Chairman of the Boundary Commission in August 1947 was arbitrary in nature, it is not without reason to suggest that a man whose previous cultural experiences had been confined to western Europe, may not have been an obvious candidate for this task. It may be argued that the decisions which led to partition were not his, and that he was ill-chosen to take upon his own shoulders an impossible role that enabled others to abdicate their responsibility for the massacre that was to follow. Given just five weeks to complete his mission and with no real insight into the socio-political context in which he was working, it is hardly surprising that many today quite understandably regard him as a figure of contempt. In mitigation for an act undertaken, which was clearly beyond his comprehension or capabilities, it is believed that he refused to accept the £3,000 fee for this work (£3,000 was a vast sum of money in 1947).

The establishment of a boundary and with it the creation of a new country resulted in the movement of around 14 million people and the mass slaughter of possibly as many as 2 million, as has been well documented in many tragic personal accounts and histories of this period. Perhaps as great a tragedy is the fact that since this time the levels of enmity between the two independent countries of India and Pakistan has resulted in major armed conflicts in 1965 and 1971, and the more limited Kargil war of 1999. Even today, those occasions when I can pick up a newspaper during my regular visits to India without seeing reports of further border skirmishes, are indeed rare and it seems that the politicians of both India and Pakistan have little idea of how they might resolve the ongoing tensions which exist between these two powerful countries.

I was recently at a conference in Delhi, attended by delegates from across the region, though notably none from Pakistan. During this event I found myself one lunchtime in discussion with a colleague from a university in Dhaka, Bangladesh. During the course of our conversation we both expressed our regrets that an absence of Pakistani delegates made the conference feel in some ways less representative of the South Asia region. At this point I recounted the tale of my student whose grandmother had been born an Indian and was now officially a Pakistani. My Bangladeshi colleague shrugged his shoulders and told me, this is nothing, reporting that his grandmother was also born in India, she then became Pakistani and is now a proud citizen of Bangladesh. Apparently, she was born in Chittagong in 1941, became a Pakistani living in what was then East Pakistan in 1947, and a Bangladeshi in 1971 after what is usually referred to as the Bangladeshi Liberation War. It is to be hoped, stated my colleague, that matters are now stable, and she will not be expected to adopt a further nationality.

The Israeli writer Amos Oz in his 2014 novel Judas described the creation of boundaries as a major source of many problems. Once one draws a line of demarcation to establish a border he suggests, the people on either side stare across the divide and see that which they believe to be exotic. They are in effect like visitors to a zoo. They seldom see those characteristics that bind us together, but are more inclined to emphasise difference, and once those differences are established we compare them with our own experiences and often measure what we see as inferior to what we know. Oz was of course referring to the disputed border between Israel and Palestine, but he could equally have been discussing that which exists between India and Pakistan, North and South Korea, or many of the other troubled parts of the world.

In what ways has my former student's grandmother changed since she became a Pakistani? Has the transformation from Indian to Pakistani and finally to Bangladeshi fundamentally altered the humanity of my colleague's grandmother? I suspect that the person behind the label has not greatly changed, though the politics and environment, which have shaped the lives of both of these ladies, have had a significant impact upon how they are perceived both within and beyond the borders of their nations.

According to Plutarch's text *Of Banishment*, Socrates is credited with having said, *"I am not an Athenian or a Greek, but a citizen of the world."* I suspect that when he made this assertion there were few in Greece, or for that matter in Macedonia, or the great civilisations of the Pallavas or the Chola in India who would have seen the world in his terms. I am convinced that the levels of jingoism that characterise much of today's politics mean that we have made little progress in our thinking since the days of Socrates. Would it be possible for one of the world's most powerful men to propose the construction of a wall between two countries had we made such an advance? I am however heartened, that students from Pakistan continue their studies in England, that my colleagues from England work alongside others from China, Brazil, Iraq and Turkey and that Bangladeshi academics meet with others from Australia, the UK, India and Korea in conferences where they can enjoy each other's company and recognise what they can learn from each other.

What we have in common is a shared humanity, that which divides us has generally been created by those who are afraid to recognise this as a fact. Will this ever change? Sadly, the physical borders that have been created between nations are destined to remain, but perhaps we could do more to dismantle those artificial boundaries that have become embedded in our minds.

Murder is Just that, No Matter How it is Portrayed

What do John Wilkes Booth, Lee Harvey Oswald, James Earl Ray and Nathuram Godse all have in common? Apart from the obvious answer, that they were all cold-blooded murderers of prominent internationally known figures, I would suggest that they were also pathetic individuals; unknowns who gained notoriety only through a violent act of assassinating individuals whose names were familiar to millions across the globe. Each one through an act, which took no more than seconds, assured that their names would be written into history, and that they would gain notoriety not for some deed of great heroism, or as a result of noble achievements, but simply because they chose to destroy the life of an individual whose contributions to society were many, and revered by significant numbers of the population.

Now let me ask a different question. What is a significant difference between John Wilkes Booth, Lee Harvey Oswald, James Earl Ray and Nathuram Godse? A simple, but I suspect to many people surprising answer, is that of these murderous assassins only Nathuram Godse has come to be held in reverence by a small but significant number of individuals and groups, who have appropriated his sad character to represent their misinterpretation of history and to perpetuate their own political agenda.

In recent years statues and busts, many of them poorly manufactured and only a few of which bear any true resemblance to Nathuram Godse, whom they purport to represent, have been unveiled in several parts of India. As an example; in November 2017 the Hindu Mahasabha unveiled a shiny, though not terribly life like bust of Gandhi's assassin at their Gwalior Office, whilst also announcing their intention to plan a temple to his memory. A few years ago, the production of a film *Desh Bhakt Nathuram Godse* (Nathuram Godse the Patriot), which attempted to raise him to the status of a martyr, was banned by a Pune court order. Personally, I have always opposed the banning of works of art, even when these may present a viewpoint different from my own, and may be of limited creative merit, but I suspect that this particular film, along with other projects from the supporters of Godse, was intended more to provoke a reaction than to add to some great canon of artistic works.

It is of course, easy to argue that the Hindu Mahasabha is a minority organisation that represents the views of a relatively small number of Indians, many of whom have a limited appreciation of history. But that should not detract from a need to understand how one small sector of society feels it appropriate to make a martyr of an individual who committed a heinous crime.

A few years ago, I read an excellent account of the days leading up to the assassination of Mahatma Gandhi written by Tushar Gandhi, the grandson of the *"Father of the Nation"* and son of Manilal Gandhi. In his book *"Let's Kill Gandhi[1]"* the author presents a wealth of documentary evidence, court reports and eye witness accounts of a terrible crime that appalled not only the Indian public, but citizens across the world. Of course, it can quite rightly be argued that in his presentation of this tragic story Tushar Gandhi can lay little claim to impartiality; a fact with which I feel sure he would concur. Similarly, many who have written accounts of the life of Gandhi, including Narayan Desai who was closer to him than most and has left us with a most detailed biography[2], would never suggest that their interpretation of events was totally devoid of bias. But whatever views these and other followers or detractors from Gandhi's life and philosophy might believe, the simple truth is that murder is just that, an unjustifiable violent ending of the life of a fellow human being.

Can assassination ever be justified? This may not be as simple a question to answer as one might assume. In July 1944, Claus von

Stauffenberg an officer in the German army, along with other conspirators, attempted to detonate a bomb at the Wolfsschanze or Wolf's Lair as it is commonly called, near Rastenburg now situated in north east Poland. Had their mission succeeded the target of their attack, Adolf Hitler, would have been killed and the Second World War might possibly have ended sooner. Though this of course, is a matter of speculation. As every student of twentieth century European history knows, von Stauffenberg and his colleagues failed, thus forfeiting their own lives to a Nazi firing squad in the early hours of the following morning.

Few would dispute the fact that Hitler and his coterie of Nazi fascist thugs was at the head of despicable and malicious gang, who brought wholesale destruction to much of Europe and beyond, and were responsible for the deaths of millions. Whether or not his assassination would have led to an earlier conclusion to the war is a point which has been subject to continuing debate. If this had been the case, would von Stauffenberg today be lauded as a hero? Would his murderous act have been justified? Quite possibly so, though this remains as a matter of conjecture, which will likely fuel debates among the historians of the twentieth first century for many years to come.

A second example of assassination, but in this instance one that did succeed, can in some ways be more closely associated with the bloody deed committed by Nathuram Godse. On 13 March 1940, at Caxton Hall in London, Udham Singh shot and killed Sir Michael O' Dwyer, a former lieutenant governor of the Punjab. As recorded in Anita Anand's well researched book *"The Patient Assassin[3],"* Udham Singh spent many years planning to take bloody revenge for the massacre perpetrated at the Jallianwala Bagh in Amritsar by Brigadier General Reginald Dyer. At the time of the Jallianwala Bagh atrocity, O'Dwyer was in his position of authority in the Punjab and along with many other representatives of the British government, sought not only to justify this grotesque crime against Sikhs going about their daily business, but also to shield Dyer from justice.

Udham Singh's anger was fully justified and to an extent understandable. The slaughter of more than 400 innocent men, women and children, who had gathered to celebrate the important Sikh festival of Baisakhi in the Jallianwala Bagh in April 1919, was never properly addressed through judicial procedures, leading to resentment and a reinforcement of negative beliefs about British justice. However, Udham Singh's revenge did nothing to alleviate the suffering of Sikh families affected by the massacre that took place 21 years earlier, and whilst he is now regarded as a hero in some quarters, to most of the world his name is today largely unknown. As with most assassins his name has passed along a trajectory from obscurity to notoriety, only to return once more to obscurity. Following the publication of Anand's book, I had a conversation with three young friends in India, none of whom were familiar with the name Udham Singh, though they were familiar with the story of the atrocities committed by Dyer in Amritsar.

Since the murder of O'Dwyer in 1940, many more assassinations of prominent leaders and heads of state have been committed. Liaquat Ali Khan (1951), John F. Kennedy (1963), Robert Kennedy (1968), Anwar Sadat (1981), Indira Gandhi (1984), Rajiv Gandhi (1991), Benazir Bhutto (2007); the list goes on. In most cases the identity of the perpetrators of these terrible crimes are forgotten long before those who were killed. There is of course, a very good reason for this. In the eyes of most decent human beings, the assassins are villains who have committed one of the most dreadful of crimes; that of taking away the lives of those whose opinions stood in opposition to their own. Let me be clear, I am not making a point in favour of the policies of any of those listed above, but certainly I am appalled by those who saw violence as a justifiable means of silencing them.

In democratic societies the rule of law and due diligence on the part of those charged with its administration, provides a well-respected and appropriate system for bringing the perpetrators of criminal acts to justice. In such democracies the opportunity to elect political representatives ensures that leaders and officials can be held to account through a fair and transparent system of elections. Whilst it is true to say that all such democracies are flawed, as things stand they still provide the best means of ensuring equity and justice that we have managed to establish thus far. Democracy has emerged as a system based upon a desire to see fair play, with recognition that whilst we may not always agree with the ideals of our elected representatives or the parties that they lead, we will at least have an opportunity to hold them accountable for their actions every few years.

In the world's strongest democracies free speech is encouraged and allowed to flourish. Whilst dissidence may be uncomfortable for those in power, it is recognised as an essential element of the process of debate and interrogation of ideas that enables justice and democracy to thrive. Those of us who hold these principles dear have at times taken to the streets to protest those actions, which we perceive to be an infringement of rights, or a challenge to the freedoms that have often been won only after significant historical struggles.

Throughout the first half of the twentieth century many courageous individuals from all communities across India protested the pernicious imperial rule of my countrymen. The successes achieved by great leaders who united the vast majority of the Hindu, Moslem, Sikh and secular communities throughout this period, stand as a tribute to the possibilities of bringing about change through a unified approach. Great Indian community leaders such as Muhammad Ali Jinnah, Tara Singh and Vallabhbhai Patel often had their differences, but were all committed in opposition to British rule and their desire for independence. At various times each of these significant figures looked to Mahatma Gandhi for inspiration, including on those occasions when they did not necessarily agree with his strategies. This even included his detractors, who at least recognised that he above all Indians had the ability to unite activists from across the political and religious spectrum. Gandhi remained a devout Hindu, even proclaiming his faith with his last utterance as he fell to the earth having been shot three times in the grounds of Birla House in Delhi. He also proclaimed the rights of those of other faiths and none, to be recognised as Indian citizens.

The importance of unity in creating the conditions for freedom was tragically forgotten too soon after the establishment of Independent Indian and Pakistani states in 1947. The cataclysm of partition, which resulted in the deaths of so many innocents from the Hindu, Sikh and Moslem communities fleeing their homes, and the bitter wrangling between political and religious leaders, created a climate of untruth and disaffection that ultimately resulted in the assassination of Gandhi, by a man who was manipulated by others for their own iniquitous purpose.

Nathuram Godse as the perpetrator of a savage crime was in some ways himself a victim. Many of those who had encouraged him to assassinate Gandhi denied their part in the plot and distanced themselves from Godse immediately after the event. There have been suggestions that Godse throughout his life suffered some form of traumatic mental illness related to his upbringing. Manohar Malgonkar in his book *"The Men Who Killed Gandhi*[4]*"* relates stories from Godse's childhood and aberrant parenting, which he believes may have left him with complex personality problems. There is much speculation around the character of this man, but what is known is that he remained defiant and attempted to justify his actions, even as he went to the gallows at Ambala Jail in November 1949.

There can be no doubt that Mahatma Gandhi would have been a vociferous opponent of the death penalty that was meted out to Godse at his trial in the Punjab High Court in Shimla. Gandhi regarded the life of every individual as sacred and would have rejected any suggestion that his assassin should be excepted from this belief. Indeed, Gandhi's sons Manilal and Ramdas, sought to have the death penalty overturned, but their objections were overruled by Nehru and his immediate cabinet associates.

Statues of Mahatma Gandhi are to be found in cities across India and beyond. In London, Tavistock square has become a sight of pilgrimage to Fredda Brilliant's beautiful memorial to the Mahatma for many devotees of Gandhian thought, and provides a focus for celebration of his life on 2nd October each year. Whilst memorials in the UK commemorate individuals who we now understand were guilty of the perpetuation of crimes committed during a period of colonial imperialism, such as Cecil Rhodes, it seems inconceivable that there would be an agreement today to erect a statue to a known murderer.

There can be no doubt that Gandhi would have been appalled by the execution of Godse. He would have been amongst the first to say that those who have opinions that differed from his own had every right to express these. He would undoubtedly have expected that his assassin should face justice through the courts, but he would never have condoned the issuing of a death penalty. The installation of a statue in tribute to a murderer in the country that he loved, and for which he worked for so much of his life, would also have horrified Gandhi. Yet I believe that he would have been equally opposed to the raising of expensive memorials to himself, when the work that he began in hope of creating a more just and equitable society, has failed to achieve the results that he desired. When we erect memorials to the departed we do so for the sake of those who remain, possibly more so than as a tribute to the dead.

Those who have chosen to commemorate the lives of an assassin are probably deserving if not of our sympathy, then perhaps a little understanding. They have elected to celebrate an event, which for most decent and reflective people across the world remains as one of the most shocking crimes of the twentieth century. In their attempts to portray Nathuram Godse as a martyr, they are reinforcing the failure of evil to triumph over human goodness, and to reject violence as a means of solving the problems that still confront all of our societies. Such men are clutching at straws. Perhaps we should throw them a lifebelt.

[1]Tushar A. Gandhi. *Let's Kill Gandhi: A Chronicle of his Last Days, The Conspiracy, Murder, Investigation and Trial.* Published by Rupa in 2007.

[2]Narayan Desai. *My Life is My Message. A biography of Mahatma Gandhi.* Translated by Tridip Suhrud. Published by Orient Black Swan in 2009

[3]Anita Anand. *The Patient Assassin: A True Tale of Massacre, Revenge and the Raj.* Published by Simon and Schuster in 2019

[4]Manohar Malgonkar. *The Men Who Killed Gandhi.* Published by Roli Books in 2008

Morning Raga

An early start this morning, despite this being a day of rest before six intensive days of teaching in Jayanagar. A short drive across town with friends took us to Kumara Park where a considerable crowd was gathered awaiting a morning performance. A colourful throng of individuals and families, each seeking a position that afforded a view of the temporary stage was milling around a large open ground sheltered on all sides by elegant trees. The sun not long having risen, many were wrapped in shawls or wearing sweaters that I am sure they will discard as the day progresses. Eventually the crowd settled, seated on rocks, balanced atop a small gazebo type structure, cross legged on the floor, perched on top of short walls, or in some cases sprawled on blankets spread across the ground. All had jostled politely for the best available vantage of the temporary stage and now waited expectantly for the spectacle to begin.

A brief announcement and the musicians arrived, welcomed warmly by an audience several hundred strong. The brothers Pandit Rajan Mishra and Pandit Sajan Mishra, internationally feted for their interpretation of classical Hindustani song accepted the welcoming applause of the crowd with great humility before settling as their fellow musicians tuned their instruments.

The morning's performance began with a song in tribute to Saraswati at first a doleful meditative tune that eventually journeyed into complex rhythms led by the tabla. The crowd tapped and danced their fingers in a poor effort to replicate the beat, swaying gently to the tune. Many sat eyes closed appearing lost within the music, whilst others stared in awe at the mastery of the maestros before them on the stage. Saraswati, a Hindu deity of knowledge and music – hopefully, I thought, this is a good omen for the week of teaching ahead.

Throughout the concert disreputable monkeys asserted their ownership of the surrounding trees. Showing little appreciation of the music, they sought the attention of the audience like naughty children by shaking branches so that we were often showered in leaves and seeds. Unable to gain sufficient respect or distract the audience from their focus on the music they plotted further mischief. By the midway point of the concert they were clearly annoyed at having been upstaged by the musicians and took to the edges of the stage to steal the flowers so carefully arranged to enhance the aesthetic of the podium.

With some humour the musicians announced that the final song would tell a story of Hanuman the monkey king hero of the Ramayana. With this the villainous malcontents affronted by what they clearly regarded as an outrage, rattled the trees, as if in imitation of Hanuman's army. I am convinced that if Sita had been dependent upon this troupe for rescue she may well have been sadly disappointed and Rama would have returned home broken hearted.

The concert over and the musicians affectionately acknowledged, we were in need of a late morning breakfast. A suitable venue was recommended by friends and we left the park with appetites heightened by the early start and the energy of the music. A short drive and we arrived at our breakfast destination. Koshy's Parade Café is a remnant of British occupation. Being in the cantonment area near Mahatma Gandhi Road it was apparently a favoured haunt of soldiers coming off parade. The owners have maintained its 1940s décor and the walls are hung with fading images of buildings from Bangalore's colonial past. It was easy to image how the room may have looked when filled with British soldiers sitting beneath the ceiling fans seeking refuge from the heat. Today it feels like a statement of post 1947 pride, recalling past oppressions but retaining its status as a venue built upon hope and tradition. The apom served with an Indian stew followed by good South Indian coffee made for a fine end to a memorable morning, surpassed only by the excellent company of the good friends with whom it was spent.

Meet me at Koshy's for Breakfast

There are many stories about famous people who may (or possibly may not) have dined at Koshy's. They include Jawaharlal Nehru, and Nikita Kruschev as well as a host of artistic and literary figures. The breakfast at Koshy's is legendary with a wide choice of both Indian and English dishes available, all served with panache and in an atmosphere, which somehow manages to bridge old colonial days and free India in a unique and lively setting.

In recent years the historian and writer Ramachandra Guha who is a regular visitor to the restaurant has used the venue to launch his books. In 2018 I met him there over a cup of coffee and along with most customers present we attempted in vain to put the world to rights. Despite its reputation as a meeting place for the local intelligentsia there is a lightness about Koshy's that seems almost to demand a simple doggerel response to its atmosphere.

Meet me at Koshy's for breakfast,
The idlis there are so fine
And the coconut chutney and sambar taste good
and south Indian coffee or cardamom chai,
Whichever you choose are divine.

I'll treat you to breakfast at Koshy's
On Sunday when friends often meet
To discuss and debate all the news of the day,
Or the books that they've read or the films that they've seen
Before onset of the day's savage heat

Once you've had breakfast at Koshy's
An experience that should not be denied,
You will come back again for the fare and the banter,
To share in the gossip, to hear all the scandal
That Koshy's alone can provide

The Dignity of an Unheralded Artist on the Streets of Bangalore

For two consecutive days when returning to my accommodation after an early morning walk I cursed my ill-fortune at having missed an opportunity. Determined to make amends, on the third morning I started my brief sojourn of the streets of Jayanagar in Bangalore forty minutes earlier than usual, and stepped out with greater purpose than before. 5.30 am is a good time to explore the lanes of the city on foot. It is only at this point in the day the pedestrian is afforded a rare opportunity to walk in relative safety, before the chaos that constitutes the traffic of this vast metropolis has bludgeoned every walker with the least regard for personal safety into submission. It was therefore with some confidence that I made my way through the labyrinth of lanes which spread like tentacles from the main thoroughfare through the urban sprawl of this city suburb.

Usually on these dawn excursions my wanderings are fairly aimless, following no regular pattern and having the sole objective of exploring the area in order to gain my bearings and take some exercise before the commencement of a day's work. But on this particular occasion I was more focused and set out on a quest; hopeful of discovering an artist at work and with any luck to witness creation in progress, rather than simply viewing the results of the creator's labours. Whilst I had every confidence of locating the venue where today's masterpiece was likely to be found, I was less assured that my timing would enable me to view the artist whilst engaged in the act of producing her work of art. But, as is the case with many journeys, I set out full of hope if not expectation.

Rangoli patterns comprising a series of flowing whirls and geometric motifs are a common enough sight on the pavements and thresholds to be found in the backstreets of Bangalore, as they are in other parts of India. On many occasions I had stopped to admire the intricate swirls and interweaving patterns produced by the women who fashion these elaborate designs. There had been instances when I had caught a glimpse of an artist, bent double from the waist putting the final touches to her work, but as yet I had failed to observe the whole process, from the first outlines made precisely with the delicate placing of the red ochre sindoor stained flour, to the completed geometric shapes flowing from the delicately placed utswdhermita, which signify a conclusion to the process. Wishing to address this omission in my experience of Rangoli production and knowing that these skilful women work quickly, I made my way to the narrow lane where I had on the previous two mornings found elaborate examples of these intricate but ephemeral works of art. Timing is critical to those who wish to find these pavement Rangoli designs, which within a few hours of their production are inevitably be swept from the streets by the passing of many feet as local pedestrians go about their business. Hopeful that I would arrive before the artist began her labours I took up my position and waited.

There are many myths and legends surrounding the production of Rangoli, some associated with the deity Mahalakshmi, of whom it is said that she will bring good fortune to the house outside which a woman makes a pattern whilst chanting sacred mantras. I have noticed that during festivals such as Dusshera, celebrated at the end of Navatri each year in Bangalore, there seems to be a small increase in the number of Rangoli patterns to be found on the streets. As is fitting for a festival closely associated with a celebration of the bounties of harvest, during this festival these make use of natural materials often incorporating flowers, seed pods and leaves within the design. During this period it is possible to make a circuit of the district and to see several variations in design, colour and texture amongst these traditional patterns.

But today I was in pursuit of observing a single artist at work. One who had created a design I had seen on both previous mornings, and whose intricate patterns had held my attention and fascinated me by their complexity. For this reason I arrived early at the venue and took up position across the narrow road from the house from which I hoped the lady would emerge. After ten minutes I began to feel concerned that my mission was in vain, there was no sign of an artist and I began to curse my own stupidity for having missed an opportunity on previous mornings to see an artist in action, which would clearly have presented itself had I arrived earlier during my early morning visits to this site. But just as pessimism began to gain the upper hand a lady emerged through a gateway carrying a large metal bowl, the contents of which I could not at first discern. As she took up her position on the path outside of her house I indicated to her that I wished to observe her at work and checked that she was comfortable with my presence. Her English was marginally better than my Kannada and I was therefore grateful when she smiled and indicated that she was quite undisturbed by my interest in her morning ritual.

As I watched, she began by creating an almost perfect circle of bright vermillion. This was done quickly filling her hands with powder from the large bowl which was delicately balanced on her hip and turning herself about, until every part of the circle was filled to present an even canvas upon which she could work. At this point she removed a smaller pot from within the large bowl and commenced to create an elaborate pattern using what looked to my uneducated eye, to be either sand or salt. The whiteness of this medium stood out boldly from the background red as she utilised her finger tips as a delicate channel through which to feed the powdery substance. From my vantage point some five metres away, I could see how with a simple flick of her wrist and rubbing together of her fingers she was able to vary the flow of the powder, occasionally doubling back along a line to add thickness or emphasise a shape.

Within five minutes the whole process was completed and standing upright the artist offered only the briefest of glances at her creation before gathering her bowls together and making to re-enter her house. I felt that I wanted to applaud, but was unsure whether this might be seen as disrespectful of an activity, which clearly had significance and a deeper meaning for the artist than I might be able to understand. In saying thank you, I was aware that this hardly seemed sufficient reward for the opportunity I had experienced to observe the creation of something so beautiful in its simplicity. Having heard my far from adequate thanks, the lady smiled and with a simple shake of her head, a gesture that has so many meanings here in South India, she turned and was gone.

In watching this artist at work a number of thoughts went through my mind. Firstly, I suspect that the woman I had seen creating this beautiful and clearly to her, significant image, would not apply the nomenclature of artist to herself. I would imagine that the image that she laid upon the pavement today was similar to many others that she has produced over a number of years, and that her skills had possibly been learned from her mother, and may well have been passed down through many generations. Who might define the artist I wondered? In my eyes she was the creator of a fine, if ephemeral work of art and therefore deserving of being seen as an artist. Others, including the lady herself I imagine might be surprised that I refer to her in this way, though I believe that I am fully justified in asserting that what I witnessed this morning was true artistic endeavour from an individual with skills and understanding that the majority of us could not replicate. For this reason I will not be dissuaded from the terminology that I have applied.

The nature of her work was of course ephemeral. I have no doubt that a return to the roadside gallery in which she created her Rangoli pattern a few hours later, would have found the image if not wholly erased, certainly smudged and distorted. Does this devalue the work which she so lovingly made upon the pavement? There are many instances of artists who have produced work knowing it to be ephemeral and temporary in nature. A few years ago my wife and I attended an exhibition at the Yorkshire Sculpture Park of work from the British artist Andy Goldsworthy. This included images and sculptures made from a range of natural materials including flower petals, stones, twigs and leaves, all cleverly arranged to provoke discussion from the viewers of this eclectic mixture, used to produce what were most certainly works of art. Other artists such as Richard Long, Leonie Barton and James Brunt have created images in the landscape using the resources that come immediately to hand, such as pebbles on a beach, or pine cones and leaves, which will be erased by an incoming tide or scattered on the wind. For many such artists the beauty is as much in the act of creation as it is in the finished work, but this does not lessen the aesthetic of their efforts.

In India there is a long tradition of artists creating work which sits comfortably in the environment for a time before eventually fading away. The lively images of the Madhubani paintings traditionally produced by the women of the Mithila region of Bihar, or the wall paintings of the Warli tribes in Maharashtra State were never originally intended to have the permanency that we tend to hope for in much western art. In recent years the introduction of methods and materials to assist artists from these communities to place their art on a commercial footing, has begun to change the ways in which these images are regarded. This has resulted in new opportunities for today's Indian artists such as Ratna Raghia Dhusalda, Bhuri Baï and Balu Mashe who, whilst maintaining traditional tribal approaches have gained recognition from a much wider audience. In the past the influence of such work extended to some European artists such as Picasso, Brancusi and Matisse who recognised that what others saw as simplicity in tribal works was often far more complex and imbued with meaning, and possessed an ability to communicate in ways that were largely misunderstood.

Whilst I would never suggest that the lady who granted me an audience this morning, as she produced her beautiful Rangoli could be compared directly to Picasso, I am prepared to say that they walk along a similar continuum of artistic endeavour. Both Picasso and this unheralded lady artist, recognise the value of art as a means of communication and have developed a set of skills and knowledge, which enable them to command the attention and admiration of those who care to stop and stare. Only the narrowest of minds would deny that the act of creation should not be only the preserve of those who receive formal recognition for their work.

On one final note; whilst watching the lady artist at work this morning a further impression came to my mind. As I tracked her graceful movements around the pattern that she was so deftly creating on the ground. I noted that rather than getting close to the earth by flexing her knees, all of her work was performed by bending at the waist. This image remained with me throughout the day until I suddenly realised where I had seen it before. At the first opportunity I turned to a book which catalogued much of the work of Vincent Van Gogh and searched for the series of drawings that he produced whilst living in Nuenen between 1883 and 1885. Here in Van Gogh's work I was able to refer to the collection of pictures, which honour the dignity of the peasants who lived in this Netherlands village. Many of the drawings depict women working in the fields, some of whom, just like today's Bangalorian artist are bending from the waist to work close to the ground with their hands. An image of a woman planting potatoes and another simply described as *"peasant woman bending down"* from the Kröller-Müller Museum in Otterlo could easily have been a representation of the Bangalore street artist at work on a Rangoli design.

Here then is the true value of art. In observing what many would undoubtedly regard as a simple domestic task on the streets of Bangalore, I have had the pleasure of seeing an act of creation by a lady artist whose movements have led me on a journey to consider the nature of the created image. This has included a reflection upon the coming together of western and eastern influences and the relationship between labour and beauty. Now, who will dare to tell me that the lady who I was privileged to see at work this morning is not an artist whose work deserves to be celebrated alongside that of others who assume this title?

No mere film star!

The arts and culture pages of the day before yesterday's Hindu newspaper (April 24th 2015) brought back vivid memories of my first visit to India with Sara in 2000. The cinema remains the art form of choice to vast numbers of Indians, and brightly coloured posters proclaiming the latest films can be found on almost every street in Bangalore. But it was the Hindu article headed *"A theatrical Swing"* written by Deepa Ganesh, commemorating the 87th birthday of the late Kannada film actor Rajkumar that caught my attention.

Rajkumar was a darling of the Indian screen, revered by many film goers, particularly here in the State of Karnataka from whence he hailed. Deepa Ganesh's article gave particular attention to the *"musical innocence with which Rajkumar rendered songs"* during his distinguished film career and singled him out as a unique talent. The article fairly gushes over apparently classical songs made famous by this actor, such as Manika veena from the film Kavirathna Kalidasa, and Bisi bisis kajjaya from Haavina Hede, neither of which is known to me I'm afraid, though as I will explain Rajkumar did play a particular part in my life during that 2000 visit.

Yesterday's Hindu (25th April 2015) follows up the Rajkumar birthday celebrations with a picture of thousands of pilgrims paying homage at his Samadhi, where his widow planted a neem tree and a helicopter showered the memorial with flower petals. Reading the article I wondered how many other deceased icons of modern culture are worshipped in this manner. I think the grave of the popular musician Jim Morrison, adorned with flowers and other tributes in the at Père Lachaise cemetery in Paris, (I was far more taken with the simple memorial to Samuel Beckett in Montparnasse) is the nearest phenomena I have seen to this spectacle, but it hardly bears comparison.

The reason that the Rajkumar article struck a particular chord for me relates, as indicated to a visit to South India in 2000. Sara and I were staying at Visanta Vihar in Chennai, having spent a few days visiting Mahabalipurum and other sites around the Coramandel Coast, and were due to take the train to meet our good friend Satish Inamdar in Bangalore. The plan was that we should arrive in Bangalore where I was to speak at an event, organised for local teachers and education officials. All was going to plan until we received a call advising us not to board the train, because Rajkumar had been kidnapped by a Tamil based bandit and there could well be riots that would put us in danger.

Having never heard of Rajkumar and being in complete ignorance with regards to his significance to several million film fans, we were somewhat taken aback at this turn of events. Could people really become so passionate about a star of the silver screen? Surely this notion of danger was a gross exaggeration? Actors in my own country are often lauded and their celebrity status sees hordes of devoted fans waiting for a glimpse of them as they pass by, but this sounded somewhat extreme. As things turned out, we had been well advised, and the situation did indeed turn nasty, with a significant number of violent incidents reported. A few days later matters had calmed down, though Rajkumar was held by his captors for a period of 108 days, and we were able to resume our travels and fulfil obligations to friends and colleagues in Bangalore.

As if Deepa Ganesh's article didn't provide recollection enough, another story, also reported in yesterday's Hindu newspaper further stimulated my memories. In 2000 the perpetrator of the kidnapping of Rajkumar was a notorious bandit and sandalwood smuggler named Veerappan. For many years he evaded capture, and led a band of brigands in outlandish and often violent deeds, that terrified many individuals and communities in Karnataka, Tamil Nadu and Kerala States. At one time he was wanted for the alleged murders of more than 150 people. Eventually in 2004 he was trapped and killed by border forces in a gun battle near the village of Papparapatti in Tamil Nadu. It has now been announced in the newspaper that the film director Ram Gopal Varma, who was once featured in a BBC documentary called *"Bollywood Bosses,"* has started shooting his latest movie *"Killing Veerappan"* to be released in the near future. It appears that the influence of the actor and the bandit are destined to haunt me here in Bangalore for the foreseeable future. I will certainly look out for Varma's interpretation of events surrounding the Indian bandit once it is released.

In my total ignorance, when I first visited India, other than the wonderful films made by the great artist Satyajit Ray, I knew little of the Indian cinema. I assumed that film in India was largely produced in "Bollywood." Friends here quickly disabused me of this serious flaw in my understanding, pointing out there is a rich tapestry of film making in several other parts of India, and in many different languages. I must confess that my knowledge of Indian film has not greatly increased even now, though on the advice of a Keralite friend I did watch a most enjoyable Hindi film called *The Lunchbox* starring the actors Irrfan Khan and Nimrat Kaur, on a flight home from Bangalore last year. On the advice of Oscar nominee Bombay Jayashri who I met at an event at Sankalp school in Chennai, I did also manage to track down the film *Verukka Neer* for which she composed the sound track. Perhaps I should make the effort to learn more about this distinctly Indian obsession.

Whilst my understanding of Indian film is limited, to say the least, I do appreciate the colourful posters that are used to attract local cinema goers. These adorn many of the walls in metropolitan cities and represent a particularly vivid graphic representation of Indian cinematic heroes and villains. Actors in exaggerated heroic poses often accompanied by swooning female leads appear to be a recurring theme. Gone are the days when every male lead wore a Bollywood moustache – though who ever plays the part of Veerappan in the new film will certainly require one of the bushiest "muchis" seen in Indian cinema for some time.

Perhaps one day when I have the time during a visit, I will make a little more effort and visit a local cinema to see more of the Indian film phenomena for myself. At present I am just relieved that neither Rajkumar nor Veerappan appear to be causing me any further inconvenience.

Vendors of Dignity

Trade begins early on the streets of Jayanagar. A short walk from my accommodation not long after dawn, takes me along a bustling highway to the Banashankari Temple, where lazing dogs commune in the dusty compound whilst early morning worshippers pay homage to the deities. The delicate scent of sandalwood permeates the air and small devotional lamps burn at the temple entrance. Already it is warm, though a group of a dozen or more small wizened men wearing woollen hats pulled down over their ears sit huddled under a ragged collection of cloths, retrieving the mobility of their stiffened limbs from another cold night in the open. Continuing along the road beneath the towering pillars of the yet to function metro, a concrete monolith that scars the skyline and casts an ominous shadow over the temple grounds, I weave my path between motionless sleepers on the street and traders hurrying to market, many carrying their burden of wares balanced confidently on their heads. Walking anywhere here is fraught with potential mishaps from broken paving slabs, potholes and marauding dogs, to low slung cables and wires crisscrossing the uneven pathway.

Within minutes I arrive at the first of the vendors. Piles of hairy coconuts are arranged in haphazard fashion along the roadside verges surrounded by groups of men closing deals, loading their purchases into sacks and heaving these into the backs of small vans. The quantities purchased suggest that these essential ingredients of local cuisine are destined for the many restaurants and hotels of Jayanagar or possibly even further afield. A little further along the road and an elaborately painted lorry adorned with a beautifully created peacock is being unloaded, its cargo consisting entirely of cauliflowers neatly arranged along the road's edge and already attracting critical customers who scrutinise them and offer judgements. Broad round rush and reed baskets of custard apples are being slid along the pathway by an elderly lady bent double over the task and wheezing with the efforts of her exertions. Work is often hard and begins early for these people here in Bangalore.

Many of the stalls here feature single vegetable commodities. A five metre long pile of red skinned onions, a barrow containing only garlic and another with a tangle of bhindi stand side by side, their proprietors already engaged in brisk trade. Piles of fresh and fragrant green herbs fill the air with a confusion of aromas, first one dominates and then another takes control as I walk amongst the customers who are examining wares for texture and freshness.

A covered market slows my progress as a few passages along which I must pass narrow, these often obstructed by people, boxes and the detritus of discarded sub-standard vegetables as I wind between heaps of fruit and other fresh produce. A man is dwarfed by the pile of ginger behind which he squats and a woman, giving me the characteristic Indian shake of the head and a friendly namaskar indicates a row of neatly arranged courgettes bidding me buy.

Back outside rows of barrows provide a forum for flower sellers with their carefully constructed garlands of vermillion, yellows, blues and greens. Customers mill around the brightly coloured stalls as one of the vendors fends off an over eager cow, keen to make a meal of his display. All is bustle, light hearted chatter, hand waving negotiation, head shaking and trade.

Amongst what is seeming chaos to those unfamiliar with this scene, I am struck by the immense pride that vendors take in the management of their stalls. Vegetables are neatly regimented in orderly lines and pyramids. Garlands are lovingly arranged in a manner carefully calculated to display their colours to best advantage. Stall holders delicately shift and order fruit and vegetables, eager to ensure that customers are able to evaluate their best features. These are no wealthy business men and women but are rather drawn from the poorer communities of the city. Many have pushed their barrows considerable distances arriving early to gain an advantageous pitch and a position from which they can be most easily viewed. Most are spindly limbed, short in stature and stronger than men twice their size.

These are vendors with great dignity. They take so obvious a pride in their work and delight when customers or even mere observers such as myself, take an interest in their labours. There is so much here to be admired as these noble people exhibit and barter their goods. How, I wonder, might a formal education such as that which I am here in India to advocate have impacted their lives? More especially, how much value do we who call ourselves educated place upon the knowledge, the skills and the craft that they present to the discerning eye? Here I see individuals with great understanding and a collective of traders whose combined knowledge is a source of almost certainly underestimated value.

I suspect that the majority of the vendors working here have had little more than what we would regard as a rudimentary education. Maybe with increased opportunities some of these individuals would be working in vastly different situations. Educations can be a means of liberation, but if we restrict our interpretation of its nature it could equally be limiting and create false values within our communities. I would like to propose that the service that these traders on the streets of Jayanagar give to the people of the local community is every bit equal to that of the software engineers and call centre managers who work in locations not too distant from here.

In the scene I have witnessed this morning, one that is replicated in towns, villages and cities across India and much of the wider world, I see people working with pride and dignity who use their learning for the support of their families and in order to provide an essential service to their community. These may not be educated people in the eyes of those who manage national education policies and systems, but surely we should celebrate the understanding that they demonstrate, which is beyond that held by those of us who bear the labels associated with a formal education. I hope to return here many times to show my respect for these hard working dignified people who exhibit their learning through an expert plying of their trade.

Lulled by the Lapping of Waters

The moon was absent, so we made our way beneath an ink black palette of sky punctuated by stars. Silence occasionally broken by the gentle lapping of water, or the creaking of the shallow hull was essential after our boatman, mundu clad, standing proud like a figurehead at the prow, had pointed out the family of otters twenty metres to our right. Seemingly unperturbed by our presence, with lithe grace they turned and dived, the mother gently mewing and coaxing her cubs, coaching them to gain the understanding needed to survive in the brackish domain that will be a world they will come to know well, while to us it will remain a mystery. Ever vigilant, she took up her position between our boat and her offspring, shielding them just in case her trust, built upon familiarity with the many such vessels that ply this water, should be betrayed. She needed to have no fear; we were in awe as we enjoyed the spectacle of these beautiful creatures making their effortless way across, through and under the waters.

We had come to Kadalundi Puzha after a long and stickily hot day of work in Kozhikode and the cooling breeze across the water brought some welcome respite from the Keralite humidity. Three strides ankle deep in water had taken us to the waiting craft, followed by an inelegant hauling of bodies over the lurching side to locate a seat and await the anticipated short journey of discovery. Once we were aboard our boatmen heaved and tensed against the prow, pushing against the stubborn resistance of a hull clutched by the sand and silt of the backwater's edge. Firm in its resistance the vessel at first refused to budge, but this was a familiar challenge to these fine workmen and they knew that they would have the final say in an issue rehearsed so many times before. Muscles tensed, one final grunt and shove and we were clear, our pilots leaping aboard with far more elegance than any of their passengers had managed. But then, this is their livelihood, under such circumstances motor memory kicks in, allowing these men to demonstrate the ease with which they have adapted to their marine environment.

The boat, perhaps fifteen feet in length was ably manoeuvred from the shore, each boatman leaning easily on a twenty-foot bamboo pole, digging deep into the mud to propel us with seeming ease into open waters. One afore, one astern, working in harmony with each movement, one man complementing the other. Today again I have witnessed the rhythm of labours imbued by men committed to their craft; men who work in harmony with innate communication founded upon their years of shared mission. What these men do with ease has been I suspect, fine-tuned through many years of practice. Let us never take for granted the knowledge on display that seems so simple to our innocent minds, but defines the limits of our understanding of their reality.

Settled in our seats we six companions soon relaxed, allowing the pleasure of the moment to slip over us as we recovered from the exertions of the day. Our learned boatman constantly extended our admiration for their deft skills, as whilst never ceasing from their task of propelling us forward they pointed out the many wading birds that darted back and forth along sandbanks or wheeled or darted overhead. So many waders striding, dashing or delving deep with pointed bills as they probed and hunted for a meal. At home I would have more easily identified those familiar sandpipers, shanks or turnstones, but here they are less familiar, though a single oystercatcher black and white uniformed stood out clearly from amongst the gathered flock. Herons of at least three varieties and egrets alternately strutting the shallows or standing statuesque on guard and alert for the opportunity of the catch; these were a common sight as we progressed across the black lagoon. Two Brahminy kites, birds built for acrobatics, displayed their talents as they passed above us turning and gliding on the thermals rising from the heat of the day. These are birds upon which I could so easily pass a day in viewing and feel that not a moment had been wasted.

Beneath a railway bridge, our reverie was temporarily shattered by the rumbling of a crossing train, a brief annoyance emerging from the dark. But soon the quiet was restored as our hard-working boatmen led us further from our point of departure and towards the depths of a tangled mass of roots and twisted branches that comprised a dense and darkening mangrove forest. Here the din, more welcome than that which had been made by the train was created by hundreds of roosting myna birds which appeared to be, and probably were, no more than ten feet above our heads. Despite enveloping gloom my companions could no longer contain themselves and fifteen minutes of photo opportunities became the order of the day. Whatever happens to all of these snapshots I wonder? A priceless moment at the time, caught on camera, or more likely on a phone, then stored somewhere in the mysterious ether that is the digital world.

Emerging from the mangroves we began our lugubrious journey shoreward, the captain at the helm continuing to indicate the many features of this unique and soothing waterscape. With touching spontaneity one of my companions intoned a lilting song, a tale of Malayali boatmen, his words melding with the swaying of the boat and the gentle caresses of the rippling water against the prow. My mind was taken back to a similar occasion when I had rowed two young blonde Finnish women in traditional attire across a lake near Jyväskylä as they brought tears to my eyes with their passionate rendition of Finlandia. Such moments; never to be forgotten.

Safely returned to terra-firma after a final leap from the boat and a short paddle through the waters, dispersing crabs who had thought themselves settled for the night in the warming sand, smiles and handshakes were rightly exchanged. To our splendid boatmen this was all too familiar. An everyday event negotiated as so many times before. But for us this evening has etched memories long to be savoured well after Kerala fades into the distance and I have returned home.

Truly Great Men need no Ostentatious Memorials

On occasions when I visit London and have time to spare, I prefer to find my way around on foot; it is only as a pedestrian that one can truly begin to understand the geography of a city. It may be quicker, though not necessarily more comfortable to cross the city by tube, or to hail a passing black cab, but as someone who is insatiably curious about the vicinity in which I am travelling or working, walking provides a far greater opportunity to feed my inquisitive nature.

There is hardly a street in England's capital that doesn't have something of interest to arrest the gaze, whether this is a magnificent piece of architecture, one of the many blue plaques commemorating the lives of the good, the infamous and the notorious, or a sculpture erected in memory of a hero from a former generation – some who have since become regarded as villains. Cities such as London, which have a long history and have witnessed momentous events over many centuries, invariably garner a wealth of commemorative features. Many of these appear in the tangible form of statuary or place names reminding us of past events such as Trafalgar Square and Portobello Road, or people as in Downing Street or Mornington Crescent. There is perhaps something reassuring in the knowledge that history, even in this somewhat simplistic form, continues to play a part in the shaping of our urban landscape.

Journeys to London from my home in Northamptonshire are most often made by train along the Midland Main Line that terminates at the magnificent St Pancras Station, which with its adjoining hotel based upon a design by George Gilbert Scott was built under the direction of William Barlow and Rowland Ordish and opened in 1868. From St Pancras it is but a short, and very pleasant walk to the British Museum located in Bloomsbury just across the road from the splendid London Review of Books bookshop. This is a route which I have trodden on numerous occasions and have come to know well; though almost every time the journey is taken, some point of interest which I had previously missed comes to my attention. The museum being located close to the University of London Institute of Education, where I have often had occasion to attend meetings, means that I can trace a map of my walk to this venue in my mind, and have become familiar with many of the sites of interest which mark my path along this route. The British Library, with its wonderful collections and exhibition space is within a five minute stroll of the station, and whenever time allows I find myself drawn in to its spacious foyer and halls to marvel at its displays of manuscripts or browse its book shop. Here in the courtyard before the library entrance is Edward Paolozzi's imposing sculpture of Isaac Newton based upon William Blake's watercolour image of 1795, that has the great scientist measuring the universe with a set of dividers. It is hard to imagine any more appropriate location for this magnificent reminder of Newton's genius than where it stands today looking down upon visitors to one of the world's great repositories of learning.

Crossing the Euston Road from this point the observant pedestrian once attuned to the ubiquitous blue discs placed by English Heritage, can easily find before reaching Russell Square, commemorations to such varying characters as the actor, comedian and raconteur Kenneth Williams, the romantic poet Percy Bysshe Shelley and the secret agent Yeo Thomas (apparently codenamed "White Rabbit"). This area has a long association with great writers and artists and especially members of the Bloomsbury Group that included Lytton Strachey, Vanessa Bell, Duncan Grant and E.M. Forster. Attention is drawn to the one time residence of Charles Dickens in the area by yet another blue plaque, though a house in Woburn Place once occupied by an equally distinguished dramatist and poet, the Irishman W. B. Yeats is recorded by a more simple brass plate, which I suspect is missed by the majority of passing pedestrians.

The area along this route is rightly praised for its well-maintained verdant squares, which afford some opportunity for peace and quiet and an escape from the bustling London traffic. Russell Square and Bedford Square are two of the larger of these. In nearby Gordon Square can be found Shenda Amery's sculpture of Rabindranath Tagore, erected in 2011 to commemorate the 150th anniversary of the Nobel Laureate's birth. In the same square a year later, a similar memorial was unveiled to Noor Inayat Khan, a brave Indian who worked as a British agent behind enemy lines during the second world war and was captured and executed by the Nazis. But of all these fine squares with their imposing architecture and memorials, the one which I am inclined to favour as a place for quiet contemplation is Tavistock Square, with its several commemorations to those many individuals and organisations who have worked for the cause of non-violence and reconciliation.

In Tavistock square can be seen a cherry tree planted to commemorate those innocent victims killed when atomic bombs were dropped on the Japanese cities of Hiroshima and Nagasaki in August 1945. At one corner a large grey stone with a simple inscription reminds anyone who cares to pause and read, of the courage of conscientious objectors, many of whom were imprisoned during several conflicts in modern history. Elsewhere in this quiet London park stands a profound reminder of the terror, which can still haunt our lives in the form of a small cast metal plaque that recalls the tragedy, which occurred on the edge of the square on July 7th 2005, when thirteen people were killed by a terrorist bomb. However, it is one work of art at the centre of Tavistock square which is most likely to hold the attention of many of the visitors to this leafy London suburban park.

At the heart of Tavistock Square a statue of Mahatma Gandhi, seated cross legged atop a simple hollow pedestal, commemorates the life of the great leader of resistance to British Imperial rule in India. This beautiful work of commemorative art was sculpted by the Polish artist Fredda Brilliant and was unveiled in 1968 by the then British Prime

Minister Harold Wilson. Often when I have visited this place of contemplation there have been flowers placed within the hollow pedestal upon which the Mahatma rests. On October 2nd each year to commemorate the birthday of Gandhi many visit to pay tribute here and remember the philosophy of satyagraha non-violence, which he utilised so effectively along the path to Indian independence, and through which he influenced later leaders, including Martin Luther King Jnr.

A second statue of Gandhi was installed in Parliament Square, across from the Houses of Parliament in Westminster in 2015, unveiled by the then British Prime Minister, David Cameron, and India's Finance Minister, Arun Jaitley, who were joined by Gandhi's grandson, Shri Gopalkrishna Gandhi, and Indian actor Amitabh Bachchan. This statue depicts Gandhi standing, gazing towards the parliament for which he had much respect, but whose rule he defied for much of his life. Personally, I find this memorial more austere and less symbolic of the contemplative Mahatma than that located in Tavistock square. I suspect that Gandhi would have been honoured by the placement of the first memorial but would have regarded two statues in the former capital of empire as somewhat extravagant and hardly in keeping with his aesthetic life style.

Reminders of the past are important. I believe that they can provide a focus both for memory and for honest debate about those people and events in history that have shaped our lives and the societies in which we live. They may provoke fond memories and instil national pride, but can also raise the hackles of people who oppose those actions from history, which may previously have been celebrated, but are now quite rightly out of step with current sensibilities. Witness for example the debates which have surrounded the Cecil Rhodes statue which adorns Oriel College Oxford, with demands from some, that as it represents a dark chapter of Britain's colonial past, it should be torn down as a means of offering apology to those who suffered at the hands of an often oppressive regime. Others argue that it should remain in-situ precisely because it encourages the viewer to reflect on the shameful deeds from that period of history carried out on behalf of a supposedly benevolent nation. Personally I tend towards this latter view, so long as history is properly told and the edifice is not used to glorify the atrocities committed in the name of empire. The public viewing such monuments need to be well educated about the worst aspects of history, and for that reason the provision of additional information at the site commemorating the offensive imperialist may well serve a greater purpose. After all, would we wish to see the colosseum in Rome demolished because of the barbarity of Roman rule, or the destruction of the pyramids at Giza, which were built with slave labour? For history to be accurately conveyed it requires honesty and transparency, which means recognising and attempting to learn from both the good and the evil that has been perpetrated by individuals and nations. I know that not everyone will agree with this point of view, but perhaps the virtue of living in a democracy is that we can argue such points in a civilised manner. Doubtless such debates will continue well into the future.

Whilst I am inclined to argue that those who have played a critical role in our history should be remembered, and that one effective means of ensuring this is through the construction of physical edifices such as statues or plaques, I have not always been impressed by those structures which have been erected for this purpose. The sculpture commemorating Peter the Great in Moscow, which was erected in 1997 competes in my mind with the hideous structure in Konstanz's harbour, which is said to celebrate the Council of Constance in the fifteenth century in terms of ugliness. Should both of these be removed from the public view, not that this is something I am advocating, though I suspect that there would be few who would mourn their passing.

It is, however, a far more recent structure which prompted me to think again about the place and purpose of memorials in modern day life. On October 31st 2018 in India, Prime Minister Narendra Modi proudly inaugurated the world's tallest statue. Located on an island named Sadhu Bet and facing the Sardar Sarovar Dam on the river

Narmada, the *"Statue of Unity"* commemorating the life of Sardar Vallabhbhai Patel (1875–1950) stands 182 metres tall and was built at a cost of 420 million United States Dollars, with much of this money raised by the Gujarat State Government.

I have not yet had an opportunity to visit this monument. Pictures reveal it to be a good likeness of Patel, India's first Deputy Prime Minister and undoubtedly one of the most significant leaders in the struggle for Indian independence. It is without a doubt an impressive sight and certainly represents a magnificent feat of engineering. I understand that this leviathan of a memorial has already attracted many tens of thousands of visitors and that there are plans for a new railways station to make such pilgrimages easier. I have also been told by friends who have visited that it houses an interesting exhibition celebrating the life of this significant figure from India's turbulent twentieth century.

Having acknowledged the undoubted achievements to be celebrated in the erection of this incredible edifice, I do find myself wondering why this memorial has been constructed now and what Patel himself might have thought about it. Patel has been described as the *"iron man of India,"* a pragmatic foil to Jawaharlal Nehru's idealism. During his lifetime he achieved greatly deserved recognition by standing up for the rights of Indian citizens. He was instrumental in organising relief efforts at the time when plague and famine had devastated Kheda in his native state, and was lauded for his successful campaign on behalf of the landowners of Bardoli in their resistance against increased taxes. In much of what I have read of this great man he can be seen to have empathised with people who were oppressed or marginalised, and to oppose those who wielded power over the disadvantaged sections of Indian society.

In his lifetime, in common with many other Indians who resisted British rule, Patel made great personal sacrifices in standing tall for what he believed to be right. Along with Gandhi, Nehru, Rajendra Prasad and many others he spent time in prison for his activities, and was unflinching in his resolve to confront oppression wherever it was to be found. He was undoubtedly a towering figure in the struggle for independence and in his representation of down-trodden peoples, and it is right that there should be permanent reminders of the many sacrifices he made for his country and the cause of freedom. Above all, Patel was a man of great humility who worked hard for the poorest members of Indian society and for this reason I find myself questioning the virtue of erecting this gigantic *"Statue of Unity."* I ask myself whether this is truly a tribute to a great man or simply a means of asserting the power and influence of those who have been responsible for its erection. I do so in part because I believe that Patel would have found himself in accord with those local tribal leaders who boycotted the opening of this monolithic memorial, suggesting that it had led to the destruction of precious natural resources and significantly impacted their way of life. Patel was renowned for listening to the voices of such people and would be uncomfortable that they feel that their right to be heard had been largely ignored. I also find myself wondering about why a memorial to an undoubtedly great man needed to be lauded in the language of the competitive market place. Much has been made of the fact that this is, for now at least, the tallest statue in the world. Indeed more column inches in the Indian press have been devoted to this fact than to discussions of the many great achievements of Vallabhbhai Patel.

I am certainly not opposed to the idea of memorials and I feel that it is only right that those individuals who have given great service to their nation and to humanity in general should be commemorated with structures, which can have a degree of permanence. Since 1955 Patel's life and achievements have been commemorated in an annual lecture broadcast on Indian national radio. Eminent speakers at this prestigious event have included the independence activist, writer and politician Dr. Rajagopalachari, the scientist and former President of India Dr. Abdul Kalam, and the eminent historian Dr. Romila Thapar. Institutes of technology in Mumbai, Vasad and Surat, the International Airport at Ahmedabad and a university at Vallabh Vidyanagar have all been named in honour of Patel's achievements and his contribution to the country. These are certainly fitting memorials to a man who served India and its people with great humility and determination over many years.

Memorials serve a great purpose. They enable us to reflect upon the lives of those who have worked for improvements in the status and condition of others. Thus, when I visit London I am pleased to pause and reflect on issues of social justice and human rights when I stand before the memorial to Mahatma Gandhi. In the same location I can view the sculpted bust of Virginia Woolf and recall that she reminded us of the beauty of words when she stated that *"language is wine upon the lips."* In a matter of minutes I can stroll across to Gordon Square where the bust of Tagore brings to mind the rhythms of Gitanjali or the beautifully crafted memorial to Noor Inayat Khan mentioned earlier that reminds me of the courage shown by those who stood against fascism in the twentieth century. Each one of these monuments serves to value the lives of those who have influenced the ways in which we view the modern world. Such works of art can enhance the environment as well as honouring the figures that they commemorate.

I can't help feeling that such tributes can be achieved in ways far less ostentatious than building the world's tallest statue. After all, in the macho world of international politics it is only a matter of time before someone will take up the challenge of constructing one that is still taller. History will show that Patel stands proud in the annuls of Indian and world history and it is likely that his contribution to humanity will remain long after any of the statues erected to his memory have decayed. Can the same possibly be said of those who wish to bask in his reflected glory by erecting the world's tallest folly?

Afterword

"The love of one's country is a splendid thing. But why should love stop at the border? There is a brotherhood among all men. This must be recognised if life is to remain. We must learn the love of man.

Pablo Casals

The consequences of erecting barriers and constructing borders has been at the forefront of my thinking throughout the years during which I have assembled this selection of writings. Throughout this period, I have often found myself questioning the purpose and nature of some of the borders, both physical and psychological, which have become the focus of conflict and the cause of marginalisation in the lives of many people.

Of course, there always have been natural borders that have delineated the landscape and formed a barrier between nations and people throughout history. Living on a small island off the main land mass of Europe it is obvious that the English Channel (or La Manche as it is known to the people of France), The North Sea, and the Irish Sea, have created a natural barrier between mainland Britain and surrounding neighbouring countries. Similarly, the mighty Himalayas form a formidable border between Bhutan and Tibet, just as the Ravuma River separates Tanzania and Mozambique, and the Ban Gioc or Detian Falls on the Guichun river stand between Vietnam and China. However, in many instances the borders that are used to define some of today's nations have been constructed in recent history, often following conflict or political upheaval.

Within recent memory, the creation of two countries from one with the construction of a border to divide South Sudan from Sudan in 2011, or the earlier creation of the Czech Republic and Slovakia, from the former Czechoslovakia in 1993, are examples of the shifting nature of boundaries, and in many instances the imposition of new national identities on whole populations of people. Perhaps the most extreme example of this is the creation of Pakistan and Bangladesh from existing territories of India, with the consequent shift in national persona as I discussed in *Looking Beyond the Boundaries* in this collection. The consequences of such changes to borders can be considerable on both a national and personal level as I have attempted to portray in the short story *The Elephant Brooch*. Borders are often created for political expediency, with only secondary consideration given to those who are most affected. A consequence of empire domination has at times been the creation of borders whose impact upon other nations is great even after the colonial rulers have departed.

It would be a mistake to believe that all barriers take the form of physical borders. Throughout history there have been many examples of where it has been necessary for individuals or whole communities to struggle against oppression in order to overcome obstacles that limit their opportunities or stand in the way of their rights. Discrimination on the basis of gender, sexuality, disability, religion, caste, class or race has been, and continues to be the source of many of the barriers to progress that have impeded whole communities of people. Such debilitating factors have provided me with opportunities for reflection throughout this book. One of my historical heroines, Sylvia Pankhurst (a far more radical and interesting woman than her mother Emmeline or either of her sisters), fought bravely for the rights of women and other oppressed communities well beyond the remit of the suffragist movement, and yet there are still many barriers that limit the educational opportunities afforded to girls - an issue that I have highlighted in *Educating Manju*. The parents of children with disabilities across the world continue in their efforts to gain access to appropriate education, a theme visited in *A School for All*. In other stories I have sought to address those stereotypes that surround, poverty, language and sexuality, and have considered the influence of behaviours that continue to limit the life chances of many individuals by establishing barriers.

An intention throughout my writing of this book, has been to highlight the dignity of the many people whom I have met during my time in India. The street vendors, rickshaw drivers and market stall holders who take great pride in the services that they offer to their communities, the creativity of artists and musicians, and the skills of those who maintain traditions and celebrate the culture of a nation. Such individuals have much to teach us about humanity and the contributions that they make to ensure that society continues to function and thrive. Creativity never has been the preserve of the educated middle classes, though those from humbler backgrounds are often disregarded and their talents overlooked.

Inevitably when considering the health and conditions of a nation and the challenges emanating from those barriers that remain, some observations lead one to a position of intense discomfort. The jingoism that surrounds extreme forms of nationalism and the misrepresentation of history, resulting in oppression and the marginalisation of some groups should not, and must not be ignored. I am aware that by expressing strong opinions in a few of the articles in this book I may raise the hackles of those whose ideologies differ considerably from my own. I offer no apologies for this but suggest that democracies thrive, and barriers come down, only when debate is encouraged, and we are prepared to learn by listening to each other and respecting differences. In his seminal work "Why I Write", George Orwell (another of my heroes) reminds us that *"No book is genuinely free from political bias. The opinion that art should have nothing to do with politics is itself a political attitude."* Whilst personally holding no membership card for a political party, I concur with Orwell's view that we must never shy away from speaking what we perceive to be truth to power.

I am not greatly in favour of making predictions. Throughout history there have been far too many false prophets and Cassandras, and their contribution to society has been at best limited. However, I do not feel it necessary to hold a crystal ball, or to seek patterns in seaweed in order to express some apprehensions related to the likely future instability of national borders.

Today, as I sit in my study writing this afterword piece, I can reflect upon the meeting of world leaders that recently took place in Glasgow Scotland. The United Nations Climate Change Conference, better known as COP26 resulted in a number of commitments made by heads of state to address the critical issue of global warming and climate change. This, without doubt the greatest danger facing the modern world, is an issue that requires international action that transcends political ideologies and national borders. A failure to act will undoubtedly have a catastrophic effect.

Rising tides will soon mean that some island states will be swamped and will cease to exist. Even major coastal cities in some of the world's wealthiest countries are likely to disappear. The result of this will be the creation of a homeless population probably numbering millions. Each one of these people will be labelled as a refugee and will need to seek sanctuary in those countries that are less affected. The movement of refugees across borders has already increased during the past decade, but the current numbers are small compared with those who will need assistance in the future. Our attitude towards the dispossessed will determine whether the leaders of the world can work together to find solutions based upon greater equity, or face the possibility of a catastrophic break down of society.

The tragedy that is already unfolding has witnessed families freezing at the razor wired borders of Eastern Europe, while others lose their lives while attempting to cross the English Channel or Mediterranean Sea in flimsy boats. Each one of these is a victim of poverty, oppression, violence and neglect. In many instances their dignity has been stripped from them and they face an uncertain future dictated by powerful people who may be perceived as not caring, or at least not caring enough. Political leaders have in many instances hardened their hearts to the plight of innocent Syrians, Afghans, Rohingya, Iranians, Iraqis and

Sudanese people and those from other nations who find themselves displaced through no fault of their own. The rhetoric of politicians has been founded upon a determination to protect borders and defend nationality, at times with little concern for those whose boundaries have either become prison walls or have been totally obliterated. When I hear the Prime Minister of my own country suggesting that we need to "take back control of our borders," and a Home Secretary advocating that we should push back those boats of desperate people arriving in British waters, I cannot help but feel that some aspects of our common decency has been seriously eroded.

Writers and artists cannot ignore this situation. The author Salman Rushdie, who has himself faced the dangers and challenges of a barrier imposed upon him by ignorance and bigotry, has written of the four roots of the self. These he defines as language, place, community and custom. For those who are displaced from their homelands and find themselves in an alien culture, these four roots assume a greater significance, but are frequently undermined. Having crossed a physical border from one country to another, many refugees are forced to confront further barriers as they attempt to adjust to the expectations of local languages, community expectations and customs. Those who overcome these challenges generally go on to make a significant contribution to their adopted countries.

The Chinese artist and social activist Ai Weiwei in creating a series of works, such as his "Law of the Journey" a 230-foot inflatable boat containing 258 faceless life-size figures, "Good Fences Make Good Neighbours," a series of fences erected in New York, titled following the mischievous misinterpretation of Robert Frost's poem by an ill-informed American politician, and his powerful documentary film "Human Flow," has drawn attention to the consequences of turning our backs on the plight of desperate people who having reached a border find themselves confronted by a man made barrier. Here again is an individual who having faced oppression resulting from the imposition of barriers, has used his experiences and his immense artistic talents to challenge those who lack the ability to share in the joy of diversity.

The exclusion of people invariably results in desperation and ultimately ends in conflict. If this is to be avoided, it will be necessary to reconsider the nature and purpose of the borders that have been created, in some instances over many centuries. It has often been assumed that barriers are erected to keep safe those who shelter behind them, but increasingly it is apparent that all too often they are being used to deny a similar level of security to those who can only stand beyond the borders and focus their saddened gaze more in desperation than with hope.

Richard Rose

December 2021

Acknowledgements

This book would not have been possible without the support of friends and colleagues in India, far too numerous to list here. Suffice to say, that I have always been afforded the warmest welcome wherever I have travelled in the country. I have been fortunate to work with consummate professionals and to spend time with many people who I now feel privileged to call friends. Editorial colleagues at Cyberwit Books have been supportive and enthusiastic about my work throughout. I have also received the love and support of my family and particularly Sara who has on a couple of occasions experienced Indian hospitality when travelling with me.

Earlier versions of some of the pieces published in this book have appeared in literary magazines and other publications. I am grateful to the editors of these for expressing an interest in my work.

Anil's Reward – published in *Indian Periodical*

The Elephant Brooch – published in *Muse India*

The Missing Hero - published in *Indian Periodical*

Incident on Platform 2A – published in *Muse India*

Educating Manju – published in *Indian Review*

A Guest in Poonchera – published in *Coldnoon*

Sanjay Van: An island prison, or respite from a high-rise hell? – published in *Coldnoon*

Death of an Ambassador, If I really must go shopping, there is only one place to head for, Long live the cows of Jayanagar! Morning raga and Vendors of dignity – published in *Bangalore Review*

Looking beyond the boundaries – published in *Spark*

The dignity of an unheralded artist on the streets of Bangalore – published in *Jaggery*

Author Information

Richard Rose was born in the city of Gloucester in England and now lives in the beautiful Northamptonshire countryside. As a teacher, researcher and advocate for children's rights he has been privileged to work in many parts of the world. For more than twenty years he has travelled regularly to India to work on research and development projects with teachers, families and others committed to providing access to school and effective learning for children from marginalised communities.

Richard is the author of more than a hundred academic publications and his work on education and children's rights has been translated into several languages. His fiction, poetry and essays have been published in a wide range of international literary journals and anthologies.

Praise for Richard Rose's fiction and poetry

"It is an immense pleasure to be led through an intellectual landscape by a guide so competent, assured and unobtrusive that you forget he is there, and imagine that the power of the reaction you experience is the product of your own perspicacity."

David Gardiner, author of the novel "Engineering Paradise"

"It's funny, thought provoking, erudite and entertaining in equal measure. But above all it is poignant – the outline of Lucia's tragic life is laid bare, alongside that of her illustrious father's [James Joyce's] attempts to cope with it."

Irish Post November 2020, on "Letters to Lucia" (Richard Rose and James Vollmar).

"Rose blends place into struggles and existence of the location, philosophical thoughts and perhaps real-life happenings that define the poem itself. It's an impressive use of balance in presentation...These poems rejoice in their discoveries of place. They will show the reader a life lived fully in each one."

L.B. Sedlacek, author of "Words and Bones" on "A Sense of Place"

Printed in Great Britain
by Amazon

75995570R00132